THE **KEY** TO THE
INDIAN

LYNNE REID BANKS

THE KEY TO THE INDIAN

AN AVON  CAMELOT BOOK

I dedicate this book to today's People of the Longhouse.

AVON BOOKS, INC.
1350 Avenue of the Americas
New York, New York 10019

Text copyright © 1998 by Lynne Reid Banks
Interior illustrations copyright © 1998 by Avon Books, Inc.
Interior illustrations by James Watling
Published by arrangement with the author
Library of Congress Catalog Card Number: 98-24972
ISBN: 0-380-80373-9
www.avonbooks.com

First Avon Camelot Paperback Printing: September 1999
First Avon Camelot Hardcover Printing: October 1998

CAMELOT TRADEMARK REG. U.S. PAT. OFF. AND IN OTHER COUNTRIES, MARCA REGISTRADA, HECHO EN U.S.A.

Printed in the U.S.A.

OPM 10 9 8 7 6 5 4 3 2 1

ACKNOWLEDGMENTS

Thanks to Marge Bruchac for her trenchant criticism, and to Ronald Wright for writing *Stolen Continents*, to name only the living among the authors I have studied. But especial thanks to the people who helped me most in my efforts to get things right: those Mohawks of today, who welcomed me to their reserves in Canada and let me ask a million questions and be part of their lives for a brief, but very moving, time.

CONTENTS

THE KEY TO THE INDIAN

1

Anyone for Camping?

"**O**kay, you chaps, I've got an announcement to make."

The three boys stopped eating and looked up. Adiel and Gillon exchanged puzzled glances. It was the "you chaps" that did it, together with their father's hail-fellow-well-met manner. He simply was not the "you-chaps" type. But stranger was to come.

"What would you say to us all going camping?"

Adiel dropped his jaw. Gillon dropped something noisier, his knife and fork onto his plate. A piece of toad-in-the-hole was dislodged and fell to the floor in a small shower of rich brown gravy.

"Oh, Gillon, don't show off! What a mess!" said their mother, irritated. "Kitsa! Leave it!" —as the cat, lurking hopefully under the table, pounced. Gillon wrested it from her and plonked it triumphantly back on his plate. "You're not planning to EAT it now?" She snatched it up and left the room with it, returning at once with a wet cloth. "What are you talking about, Lionel, camping?"

"Camping is what I'm talking about. What do you say, boys?"

Adiel said, quite gently, "Are you feeling all right, Dad?"

"Never better."

"*Camping?* I mean, are you kidding? *Camping?* You mean, on our own, without you?"

"No, no, of course not. With me."

There was a silence. Omri glanced at his mother. She had mopped up the splashes of gravy and was crouched beside Gillon, just her face showing above the tabletop as if her head had been cut off like John the Baptist's and stood among the dishes. This disquieting impression was aided by the glassiness of her eyes as she stared at her husband. The two older boys were staring, too.

Only Omri was not reacting with astonishment. He sat with narrowed eyes, only pausing for a moment before hacking into another batter-encrusted sausage. Camping indeed! That'd be the day when his dad even dreamt of such a hearty outdoor pursuit, especially after the one and only time they'd ever tried it, which had ended in total disaster on the same day it began.

Omri grinned secretly at the memory of the four of them trailing home, not from some wild moorland or forest but from the local common, after they had failed to put up the tent and the skies had opened, drenching everything including the food; this had been left exposed after Gillon nicked a premature sandwich out of the cooler and left the lid off. The sunroof on the car had also been left open. . . . Their dad, humiliated by his defeat-by-tent, couldn't say much except, "That's it, boys. Home." Their mother had been very nice—she hadn't even laughed, at least not much. It was only later Omri had stopped to wonder why there had been a casserole and five baked potatoes in the oven when she had been told they wouldn't be back for two days.

Now there his dad was at the head of the table, beaming at them, the very picture of a hearty, extrovert father. He was even tilting his chair back and rubbing his hands. Gillon snorted.

The front legs of their dad's chair hit the floor. "What, may I ask, is so funny?"

"You, Dad. Camping. You're not serious—you can't be."

"Don't you want to go, then?"

Gillon considered it. Then he said, "Would it be like last time?"

"Of course not," said their father haughtily. "That was just play-camping. You're older now and we'll do it properly—we can, now we live in the country."

Adiel said, "But when could we do it?"

"*How* could you do it?" said their mother. "You'd need a tent big enough for four, a stove, sleeping bags, and God knows what."

"We've got sleeping bags from school trips," said Adiel.

"We could buy lots of new stuff!" said Gillon.

"Anyway, where would you go?"

"From here? There are wonderful camping places in almost every direction! We wouldn't have to fall back on some suburban common."

Omri looked out of the window. It was true. All around them stretched the glorious Dorset countryside. Hills, woods, fields, rivers—and the sea, only a few miles away. It *might* be fun. The only thing was, there was something behind this. Omri knew, somehow, that this wasn't really about camping. That their father had a hidden agenda.

It *had* to be something to do with the Indian.

Only two days ago, his dad had found out.

When the family had first moved into this old Dorset farmhouse, Omri had made some makeshift shelves in his bedroom out of raw planks standing on loose bricks. In the hollows of two of these bricks, Omri had hidden his most precious possessions—the plastic figures of his friends: Little Bear, his wife Bright Stars, their baby Tall Bear, and, separately, Matron and Sergeant Fickits. They were toys now, but they hadn't always been toys. Through the fantastic magic of an old bathroom cupboard and a key that had belonged to his great-great-aunt and then to his mother, they had come to life. They'd turned into real people, people from the past whom the magic of the cupboard and the key had brought into Omri's life at various times in the last few years.

How carefully Omri had guarded his secret, and how hard it had been to keep from telling anyone! With the two people who already knew—his best friend, Patrick, and Patrick's cousin Emma—living miles away, there was no one to share it with. He dared not tell his brothers, though there'd been times when it had almost just burst out of him.

Then he'd found the Account, which had changed everything.

The Account was contained in an old leather-bound notebook, left hidden in the roof thatch by his great-great-aunt, Jessica Charlotte. Omri's mother called her her "wicked" great-aunt, and she *had* admitted to at least one pretty bad act when she'd stolen her sister's earrings and been the cause of a tragedy. She had been a singer and actress with psychic gifts, and she'd owned this farmhouse; the Account had been written on her deathbed.

From this wonderful document, Omri had learnt how the key and the cupboard had been made, how the magic had got into them. Luckily, Patrick had come to spend a half-term with him, in time to share the latest marvel—Jessica Charlotte herself, brought back from the past to sing them a music-hall song and make herself, however briefly, part of their lives.

And then, two days ago, his father had gone to Omri's room while Omri had been out, to put up the proper shelves he'd promised him, and had disturbed his arrangements and *found the figures*. He'd put them all into the cupboard and locked the door. Of course they'd come to life inside, and his dad had put a lot of twos and twos from the past together, and *realized*. And later he'd seen them, been introduced to them. And accepted it . . . It took a special kind of grown-up not only to accept magic when he saw it but to promise and swear that he'd never, ever tell a living soul.

Omri knew his secret was safe. And at last he had someone in the family to share it with.

There was a problem, though.

They'd talked about it, Omri and his dad. They'd gone out for a long walk together by the sea yesterday, and talked about it. It wasn't their problem, it was Little Bear's. Little Bear was an Iroquois Indian from the late eighteenth century. And he was in trouble. Or rather, his whole tribe was, and as Little Bear was a chief, he was deeply concerned. And when he had suddenly been magicked back to Omri's time, when the key was turned and the cupboard door opened, his first words had been: "This good! I have much need!"

(Well—his *very* first word had been "Brother!" He and Omri were blood-brothers.)

Luckily the problem, though urgent, was not something that had to be dealt with on the spot. It was an ongoing problem the tribe was experiencing, which Little Bear had tried to explain—something to do with British treachery, which made Omri puzzled and uncomfortable, though he didn't really grasp what it was all about. But Little Bear seemed to take it for granted that Omri, whom he had originally assumed to be a Great Spirit with all sorts of magic powers, would come to his help.

"We'll have to go back," said Omri as they walked along the cliff tops with the salty wind blowing off the English Channel into their faces.

"Explain to me. How does one 'go back'?"

Omri did his best. He himself had only gone back once, to Little Bear's village when it had been under attack by the Iroquois's enemies, the Algonquins.

"You have to get into something," he said. "You remember my wooden chest, the one I got in the Saturday market? The one with the name L. Bear on it?"

"L. Bear! The initials on the plaque are L.B."

Omri nodded hard. The plaque was a stone slab built into their house. It had an inscription engraved in it, signed with the initials L.B. The moment Omri had seen this, when they'd first come to look at the house their mother had inherited, he had known the house would be lucky for them. Those initials—the same as Little Bear's—always, wherever he encountered them, had a

magic significance. He told his father about this as well as he could.

"This magic of yours seems to crop up in unexpected places," said his father slowly. "L.B. L.B. It rings a bell somehow—about something else—can't place it at the moment. . . . Well, tell me more about going back."

"We found out the key fitted the lock on the chest," Omri said eagerly. "The key fits a lot of different locks. So I got into the chest, and Patrick locked it, and next thing I knew I was in Little Bear's village, in a forest clearing, just at sunset. Long ago. You see, Dad, when you go back, you're small, just like when they come to us. You have to have something to—to—"

"Inhabit?"

"Yes! To bring to life. They didn't have plastic toys back then, so I—I mean, my—my spirit or whatever bit of me actually traveled back in time—became part of a painting on the side of an Indian tent."

"A wigwam."

"No, a wigwam's something different. This was a tepee. They have animal designs painted on them. I think I was a beaver . . . or maybe a porcupine." Omri had glanced anxiously at his father, half-expecting him to laugh, but his face was entirely serious. "Animals are very important to Indians. Not just to hunt. I've read about it. Each clan— D'you know what a clan is?" His father had nodded, frowning. "Each clan has its own clan animal. Little Bear's clan animal must be a bear— I suppose. I never asked him. I expect he got it in a dream—dreams are *well* important to Indians."

"Yes. I think I knew that. But I don't think they got their names from dreams."

"Anyway, I was sort of stuck there on the outside of the tepee and then there was an attack by an enemy tribe. They set the tepee on fire and I was nearly burnt to death," he concluded as carelessly as if such an adventure happened to him all the time.

His father stopped in his tracks.

"My God! That time we came home and you had a burn on the side of your head! You made up some cock-and-bull story about a bonfire—"

"Right! Luckily Patrick turned the key and brought me back just in time. It hurt like mad," Omri remembered.

His father stood on the cliff path with the rough gray Channel behind him, staring at Omri.

"This is dangerous," he said with an air of discovery.

"Yes, it is. It can be."

"I thought it was . . . just the most wonderful fun," said his father.

"That's exactly what I thought, at first. It's not fun. Not always. It's—I mean, it's real people."

"Yes. Of course I realized that when I saw them. I just . . . I suppose I just . . ."

"It's natural, Dad. You have to kind of get into it. But things really happen. You do have to—to think ahead. You can't just—do things."

"On impulse."

"Right."

"Yes. I see that. Anything could happen. Obviously you mustn't change anything back there."

"No," said Omri with great feeling. He didn't want to even think about the time he had feared he'd changed something so drastically that he, himself, might never have been born.

They walked on slowly. Then his father said, "But your wooden chest was destroyed in that freak storm. So what could we use?"

Omri thought of telling his dad that the storm, too, had happened because of the key. But he had a strange feeling of wanting to *protect* him from too much knowledge. He might scare him and then he would back off. Not that his dad was a coward, but you wouldn't have to be one to be scared of magic that could bring a cyclone all the way from the Texas of a hundred years ago, to rampage over southern England destroying everything in its path. . . .

So he just said, "Well, it has to be big enough to hold us both. And it has to have a keyhole for the key."

"But if we were both in it together, who'd turn the key?"

"Yes. That's the problem we had before. Patrick and I could never go back at the same time."

They had tramped on for a while in silence, and at last his dad said, "This is very difficult to get your mind around."

Omri knew it. But Little Bear's urgent looks and words pressed on his brain. His dad was frowning. "We need to do some research. Read up on the history. Find out what was happening back then."

"What *is* happening."

"What *is* happening . . ." He was furrowing his brows. He looked remarkably like Omri when he did that. "It seems as if it's all happening at once. History . . . time . . . in layers, kind of. When we 'go back,' if we find a way to, we'll just—drop through a number of layers and be back in Little Bear's time." Omri thought that was a good way of putting it. "But how can we be sure of getting to the right layer?"

"That's easy. We have to either go back with Little Bear or with something of his, something that belongs to the right time and place. The magic latches on to that."

"Like a kind of ticket to the right destination."

They had walked on, frowning, thinking.

Little Bear was no longer with them. He, Bright Stars, and their baby son, as well as Matron and Fickits, had all been sent back through the cupboard as soon as they'd had a talk, right after meeting Omri's father. They'd all been anxious to return to their own time, especially Matron—a superior sort of nurse, who had been in the middle of her rounds at St. Thomas's hospital in the London of 1941. The bombing of the city in World War Two had begun, and she was frantically busy. Sergeant Fickits had been preparing for a drilling session with his trainees in *his* time, which was back in the nineteen fifties.

As for the Indians, after a short, tense speech by Little Bear (during which Bright Stars allowed Omri to hold the baby, Tall Bear, in the palm of his hand, a sensation so entrancing that Omri had frankly not listened very carefully), they had asked to be sent back, too, but with the proviso that Omri and his father should make every effort to follow them soon.

"I need *counsel*," Little Bear had said forcefully. "English change toward Iroquois friends. Many years Iroquois fight at side of English against French. Many warriors die. Now they turn from us. Our people do not understand, need chief to tell what best to do." He shook his head, scowling. "I need English man. Wise man, explain what is in English heads," he said, staring at Omri's father challengingly.

Next day on the cliff top, Omri's father said, "I know something about what the Europeans did to the Indians. It's not a pretty story. . . . I don't know what we can do to help, but if our wretched ancestors are up to some tricks, which they probably are—were—*are*, the least we can do is find a way to get in there and give the Indians a hand."

And now here they all were at the supper table and Omri's dad was gassing on about going camping. What was he up to?

Everyone was talking. Their mother was on her feet again, collecting plates with a great clatter, saying that if there really was a camping holiday in prospect, they'd better do some serious planning, not go at it half-cocked like last time. Gillon was already leafing through the Yellow Pages looking for suppliers of camping equipment, and Adiel was asking if they could go as far as Dartmoor, where they could really feel they were away from civilization. Their dad was giving every impression of being absolutely serious about the whole project. Only Omri hadn't joined in.

"When could we do it?" said Adiel, who seemed quite fired up now.

"Oh, I thought in the half-term holiday," said their father.

"Great! Let's go for it!"

"There's a firm here says they do luxury tents," said Gillon. "No point spending money on some ratty old tent that'll drop to pieces or let the rain in."

"No point spending money on some palatial tent that you'll only use once, if that," said their mother. "I'll believe all you laid-back city types are going camping when I actually see it."

"Well, you won't see it, Mum," said Adiel reasonably. "You're not coming, are you."

Their mother stopped in the doorway with a pile of

dirty plates and there was a moment's silence. Then she turned and regarded them all with narrowed eyes.

"Well now. Maybe you'd better not count on that. I happen to be the only one in this entire family who has actually had some camping experience. Oh yes!" she added as they all gawked at her. "I was quite the little happy camper when I was in the Girl Guides."

"Mum. You weren't a *Girl Guide!* You couldn't have been!" they all—even Omri—yelled.

She drew herself up. "And why not? As a matter of *fact*, I was a platoon leader. I had more badges than anyone else."

"How many?"

"Eleven and a half. So there." She turned and walked out, head in the air.

"What was the half badge for?" their dad called after her.

"Making a fire without matches," she called back. "Only it went out."

They were all silent for a moment. Then Gillon went back to the Yellow Pages. "*Five*-man tents, *five*-man tents," he muttered.

"Five-*person*, don't you mean," said their father. He winked at Omri. It was one of his slow winks, a wink that said *You and I know what this is all about*. But Omri didn't. All he knew was that he couldn't wait to get his dad alone and find out.

2

The Wrong Shape

"Of course we're not really going camping, Dad?"

Omri had managed to get his dad to himself by following him out to his studio across the lane. His father was putting the finishing touches on a large painting of a rooster. He was very into roosters since they moved to the country, but they got weirder and weirder. This latest one looked more like an armful of colored rags that'd been flung into the air. But Omri liked it somehow. It was like the essence of rooster—all flurry and maleness—rather than the boring noisy old bird itself.

"Well," said his dad, tilting his head to one side and standing back with his palette. "I hadn't planned that we should. I didn't think the boys would go for it the way they did. Never mind your mother! Really, she is full of surprises. . . ." He stepped up to the easel and put a streak of red near the top of the canvas, like a cock's comb while the cock is in flight. "So I've changed my plan. Here's what we'll do. We'll arrange that Gillon and you and I will go on a preliminary trip, a sort of dummy run, to Dartmoor to pick out a suitable site and so on, while Adiel's away at school, and then we'll do it on a weekend when Gillon won't want to come."

"Why won't he?"

"We'll fix it so he won't."

"How?"

"Watch the forecasts. Pick a very wet weekend when there's something good on the box."

"And then?"

"And then, my hearty, outdoor lad, you and I will go off together, ignoring the weather, and no one will miss us for two days, and we'll *go back* and see what the situation is."

"Ah!" So that was it. A way of getting away from home, just the two of them. "But have you thought about what we'll use to go back *in?*"

"Yes. I've thought."

"Well, what? We can hardly carry some wardrobe or chest or something big enough in the back of the car!"

His father put down the palette carefully on his paint-stained table with all its jam jars full of old brushes and its rows of squashed paint tubes. "It came to me today in the square, when I was shopping. I got a load of vegetables and I couldn't carry them all in one go so the greengrocer said he'd take the other box out for me to the car. He asked me the registration, and I told him, and it burst on me like a blinding light."

"What, Dad?"

"Go and look at it. The number plate."

Omri, frowning, left the studio and crossed the yard to the open bays, in one of which was parked the family car, a third-hand Ford Cortina Estate that his father had recently bought when their old one packed up. His eyes went to the number plate and he stopped in his tracks.

The next instant he had turned and raced back, bursting into the studio with his face alight.

"Wow, Dad! Wow and treble wow! You're brilliant!"

"No, Om. It's the magic. It couldn't be coincidence. It means we're meant to go."

They went out into the yard together and stood looking marvelingly at the old car.

The registration number was C18 LB.

"C eighteen. That's for eighteenth century, of course," said Omri's dad softly. "It's a double indicator. I never thought I could believe anything like this. But I know it's true. That's our cupboard, Omri. Our time machine."

Omri went to bed that night feeling so excited he couldn't sleep. Another adventure, and with his Indian! The adventure with Jessica Charlotte, his "wicked" great-great-aunt who had actually made the key, had been complicated and thrilling in its way, but it was more like a detective story than a risky adventure, and it had all happened here in his bedroom under the thatch. A lot of it—most of it—had happened in his head while reading the Account. Now a real, true adventure was in the offing. And his dad would be part of it!

It might be a bit of a problem, though, leaving Gillon behind.

He was really getting worked up about the camping trip. He kept calling through the thin dividing wall between their two bedrooms, keeping Omri awake more than ever.

"I'm going into town tomorrow after school and get a

camping mag. They'll have proper ads in them for gear, and articles to read and stuff."

"Mm."

"It's not true that Mum's the only one who's camped. Remember Adiel went to the Brecon Beacons with his class." Omri pretended to be asleep and didn't answer. "Omri? Remember?"

"Yeah."

"He said it was grisly," called Gillon, but with relish, as if "grisly" was good. "Rained the whole time. And he got lost in a bunch of mist and hurt his leg sliding down some rocks, and they had to hunt for him for *hours*. His teacher thought he was dead, for sure! Om?"

"Mph."

"You still awake? I've heard of lots of hikers and climbers getting lost on Dartmoor! One lot died of exposure. We'd better buy some rope and rope ourselves together. We'll need proper climbing boots, knapsacks, sleeping bags . . . maps, compasses . . . a stove. . . ." His voice finally petered out on a lengthy list of prospective purchases.

Omri was nowhere near sleeping. He was actually sitting up. He'd switched on his flashlight and was making notes. Maps and compasses . . . Could you get maps of the northeastern United States back in the eighteenth century? Sleeping bags, knapsacks, and a stove certainly sounded as if they'd be useful. If only they could take them!

He kept imagining himself and his dad in the car. They could put all the stuff they'd need in there. If you were touching a sleeping bag that was wrapped round a bunch of other useful stuff, it would all go back. They'd have to really think hard. It would be no use wanting to pop back from Little Bear's time to get something they'd forgotten.

Wait.

The car.

Omri could see himself and his dad sitting in the front seats of the car, which was parked in some remote spot, with the bundles of stuff they were going to take back on their laps, and his dad had the key, the magic key.

How to lock the car? With the window open, reach through it and stick the key in the door from outside?

Or put it in the ignition?

Omri suddenly jumped out of bed and went to where the cupboard was standing in the middle of the new shelf. The key was in the lock. He took it out and looked at it. His heart sank.

The key was magic, yes. And it was a skeleton key, that would fit a lot of locks. But car keys were different. They were a different shape. They weren't cylindrical, for one thing. They were flat.

Omri suddenly knew, without any doubt, that no way would the magic key slide into either the door lock or the ignition of their car. This wasn't going to work.

Yet there was no doubting the signs. The number plate, C18 LB, was like a summons. The car was their cupboard, all right. It was just a matter of solving this little key problem.

This called for a consultation.

Clutching the key tightly, he tiptoed through Gillon's room to the head of the stairs at that end of the house. This was a Dorset longhouse, not like an Iroquois one, but a special kind they had in this part of England, one room deep with stairs at each end, no corridors. He crept down the narrow wooden stairway, which opened into the last little sitting room at this end, that his parents had designated as a TV-free zone. As he'd hoped, his dad, who didn't like TV much, was sitting there reading.

"Dad!" Omri hissed.

His father looked up. "Hello, Om. What's up? Can't you sleep?"

"Where's Mum?"

"Watching something ghastly about hospitals. Ber-lud everywhere," he added, quoting Gillon.

Omri glided over to him.

"I've thought of something ghastlier. Look at this key. Think of the car."

His father took it from him and examined it. "Oh, *no,*" he said softly.

"See? It's not going to fit."

"Of course not! Why didn't I think of that? I was so excited about the number plate—"

Omri sat beside him on the minisofa. "What'll we do?"

They sat silently for a long time, thinking. Omri had time to notice that the book his dad was reading was one of *his* books about Indians—his dad must have gone into his room earlier and taken it from his "library." It was a huge tome called *Stolen Continents* that Omri had bought second-hand. Now it slipped to the floor and neither of them picked it up.

The whole adventure was poised on the edge of being aborted. Before it had even begun.

"You know, Omri," his father said at last, "there *is* an answer. There's got to be. The trouble for me is, I don't know enough about the whole business to find the solution. I've been thinking. That story of yours that won the Telecom prize. That was true, wasn't it—I thought at the time it had an absolute ring of truth. So I know about the first part. But a lot has happened

since then—developments. I think what you'd better do
is try to tell me everything."

"Now?"

His dad looked at his watch. It was only ten P.M. "Are
you tired? It's school tomorrow."

"I couldn't possibly sleep."

"Okay, start talking. Keep your voice down."

Omri talked for an hour.

He told about how he'd brought Little Bear back after
a year, just to tell him about his winning story, and
found he'd been wounded in a raid on his village and
left to die, and only Bright Stars going out to find him
and lug him somehow onto his pony—and then Matron,
who'd proved as good as any surgeon, taking the musket
balls out of his back—had saved him.

He told Patrick's adventure back in nineteenth century Texas, how he'd met Ruby Lou, a saloon-bar host-
ess, and how they'd saved Boone, Patrick's cowboy, from
dying alone in the desert, and how Omri had brought
them back just as a cyclone had hit the cow town and
the cyclone had come back with them. He kept remembering things and wanting to go back, or off at a tan-
gent. His father, who had had a notebook and pencil at
his side while reading *Stolen Continents*, made notes.

When Omri came to the recent part, about Jessica
Charlotte, he was getting really sleepy. His dad
interrupted.

"Listen, why don't you just give me the Account to
read for myself? And you get off to bed."

So Omri tiptoed upstairs again and fetched Jessica
Charlotte's notebook. He carried it reverently downstairs and put it in his father's hands, and stood there

while he stroked its old leather cover and ran his fore-fingers around the brass corner bindings.

"It's fascinating, almost magic just holding it," he said. "I can't wait to read this. Go on, bub, get some sleep." Just as Omri was starting up the stairs, his dad added: "Don't keep yourself awake, but do Mum's trick."

"What's that?"

"Mum says that when she's got a problem, she thinks about it last thing before she drops off. She swears her subconscious works on it while she's sleeping, and some-times in the morning the solution just appears."

So Omri did "Mum's trick." As he lay, drifting off to sleep, he thought about the two keys—the cupboard key and the car key. He laid them side by side in his imagi-nation. They were so different that anyone who didn't know what a key was wouldn't have seen a connection between them. It seemed extraordinary even to Omri, who had always taken the function of keys for granted, that something so small could make the difference be-tween being able to open a door, or make a car go, or be completely stymied.

And in this case, it was the difference between being able to go back into the past or being stuck here. Be-tween being able to have a great adventure and not. Being able, maybe, to help Little Bear in his dire trou-ble, and having to leave him and his tribe to their fate.

There *had* to be an answer. There *had* to be.

3

A Surprising Ghost

Omri woke up early the following morning. Before he'd
even opened his eyes, he "looked" at the two keys, still
lying side by side in his imagination as they had been
in his last, sleepy thoughts the night before. His body
stiffened. One of the keys had changed!

It was the car key.

He'd often seen it in reality, hanging in a box filled with
little hooks inside the front door of the cottage, where his
father and mother always hung it as soon as they came
in from driving so it wouldn't get lost. Last night, when
he'd visualized it, it had been the key he knew—a flat
metal key with a round, flat top made of some plastic
material with an *F* for Ford imprinted on it.

Now the key, as clearly in his mind as if he could see
it in front of his eyes, no longer had the round black
plastic bit at the top. It was all metal. It was as if the
whole key had been remolded.

22

He sat up sharply in bed. *Remold the key!*

How could they? And if they did, what good would it do? Only the magic key could take them back in time.

Unless—

He jumped out of bed and barged through into his parents' bedroom, which adjoined his. The door flew backward, hitting his father, who was doing the same maneuver in reverse, and nearly knocking him flying.

"Shhhh!" they both hissed, and then stifled laughter. Omri could see his mum's shape under the duvet, still sound asleep. It was far too early for her to wake up— not much past six o'clock.

Omri backed into his own room and his dad followed, closing the old-fashioned plank door silently behind them and lowering the latch so it wouldn't click. Then he turned to face Omri. He looked very tired, but his face was flushed with suppressed excitement.

"You've thought of something!" Omri guessed at once.

"We'll have to whisper. Listen." Omri now noticed he was holding Jessica Charlotte's notebook. "I read this, all of it, last night. It has *got* to be the most extraordinary, fascinating, amazing thing I have ever read. Of course I'm crazy about old diaries and stuff from the past. When I read something like this—what am I talking about, there IS nothing like this, this is *unique*, but when I was reading it I got so *caught up*, wanting to know more and more about the time she lived through, the First World War and the period before that—it was like having her right in the room, telling me—"

"Yeah, Dad, I know, I read it, I know just what you mean. But about the key."

"Yes! Well! Isn't it obvious? I mean, Jessica Charlotte *made* the magic key. She fed her 'gift,' as she called it, into it without even meaning to. Remember what she said?" He was searching through the yellowing pages and found the place, marked with a match. "Yes, here! 'I hardly knew it then—I only knew I was bending all my strength on making the key perfect, and I felt something go out of me, and then the key grew warm again in my hands as if freshly poured, and I knew it had power in it to do more than open boxes. But I didn't know what. I only knew my heart had broken and that I would have given anything *to have it be yesterday and not today.*' "

He looked up. He had a strange look in his eyes, almost as if he were on the brink of tears.

"Poor woman," he said, his voice full of pity. "You can understand it so well. She'd just seen her beloved little niece, Lottie—who was your grandmother, Mum's mother whom she never knew—for the very last time. She must've been full of bitterness and sorrow and anger against her sister for saying—well, implying—that she wasn't good enough to be with that little girl she loved more than anyone in the world. . . . You know what I figured out, Om? If a person *has* any sort of magic gift, it gets more powerful the more strongly the person's feeling. Like her son, Frederick, putting magic into the cupboard because he was so angry about plastic ruining his toy business."

"Yeah, Dad. I read it, you know."

"Om, please, don't be impatient. Let me work my way through this. You had days, maybe weeks, to read the Account and digest it. I had it all in one go and it's fairly knocked me sideways. I didn't sleep a single wink last night."

"Sorry—I didn't mean—"

"No, it's okay, it's okay. Give me a sec, and I'll cut to the chase." But his head was down—he was still turning the pages of the notebook. "It's just I'm so utterly gob-smacked about Jessica Charlotte and her story, I've half-forgotten about Little Bear. . . ." He looked up at Omri. "But, yes, the key. It came to me. Now listen. If we could find a figure, a plastic toy, that might be Jessica Charlotte—I know it'd be difficult but there can't be *that* many figures that look like her—and *if* we could, and if we could bring her forward in time, to us, we might ask her to copy the car key for us. *She* could make it magic, the way she did the other."

Omri stared at him, his brain racing. *Of course!* A slow, face-filling grin spread over his features, and he saw an answering look of incredulous delight dawn on his father's face.

"Don't tell me you've got one!"

"Yes! We've already brought her once—"

"*What!*"

"Shhh! I haven't had a chance to tell you everything. I was concentrating on Little Bear—"

"*You brought her! You've met Jessica Charlotte!*"

For answer, Omri dived under the bed and got out another of his treasures—an old cashbox, black and silver, the paint wearing off, a blob of red sealing wax still blocking the slot. He opened it cautiously. His father was so eager he was trembling. Omri carefully took out the little woman shape in the red dress with the big plumed hat, the size of his finger. His father took it from him as reverently as if it were a holy relic.

"This is her?" he whispered wonderingly.

"Yes."

"Where did you get it?"

"It was in here, in the cashbox that I found with the Account, buried in the old thatched roof. The magic key

opened it. She was fast asleep, but later I—well, me
and Patrick—"

"Patrick and I—"

"Yeah, well, she woke up, and we decided . . . I mean
it was just before she was going to steal her sister's
earrings—you know, the night she made the key. And
I wanted to change her mind and get her *not* to steal
them—"

His father's face sagged suddenly with horror. "Omri!
You didn't, did you?"

"No. Patrick said not to. Because if I *had*, it would
have changed history. Everything that came from stealing the earrings—things linked to other things, like a
chain—wouldn't have happened, and I—I might never
have been born."

His father swallowed hard. His face had gone very
pale.

"I wonder if we ought to be meddling with this," he
said at last. "I wonder if we ought not to just—just put
the key and the cupboard and the cashbox and the Account, the plastic figures and everything else, safely
away somewhere and—and just forget it."

"No, Dad! It's no use. I tried that. I did try—you know
I did—I put the cupboard and key in the bank and I
swore I wouldn't take them out and mess about with
the magic anymore, but—but you can't *not,* somehow. I
couldn't, anyway. It—when I read the Account, I—I just
felt the magic calling me."

His father was gazing at him with a very strange,
troubled expression.

"Omri. You don't suppose—"

"What?"

"Well . . . don't be scared. But Frederick obviously
inherited some part of Jessie's gift, or he couldn't have

put magic into the cupboard he made. I just wondered if that—magic power—if . . . After all, they are your blood relatives. Perhaps it's something that can be—passed on."

There was a long silence. They stared into each other's eyes.

"Wouldn't—" Omri found he had to clear his throat. "Wouldn't—Mum have had some of it?"

His father frowned and went to the window. It was framed by deep eaves of thatch. The sun was just coming up over the hill on the horizon, the one that had on its top a strange little circle of trees, like a peacock's crown.

"I suppose Mum never told you about the time she saw a ghost."

Omri jumped.

"A ghost!"

"Yes. She told me about it ages ago. I didn't believe her. Of course, I didn't believe in anything unprovable in those days."

"Whose ghost did she see?"

"Well, that's one of the things I was thinking about, lying awake last night." He looked down at the little woman shape in his hand. "I only have her description to go on, and I only heard the story once. Years ago, before we were married. She told it to me when I was saying I didn't believe in anything supernatural, including an afterlife. And she disagreed, and we were sort of quarreling. She told me this story, to prove me wrong. And I . . ." He paused, and swallowed. "I laughed."

"Tell me!"

"She said she was visiting her mother's grave—Lottie, who'd died in the bombing of London, when your mum was still a baby. Lottie was buried in the same grave as her father, Matthew, in Clapham Cemetery, near where she was born, where *her* mother still lived. Jessica Charlotte's sister."

"Maria."

His father nodded. "Yes. Maria, who brought your mother up. She was an old lady by then, in her eighties, but she went every week to the cemetery to put flowers on Lottie's grave. Mum didn't often go because she was busy with her own life by then, she was a student, but that day Maria wasn't well and Mum felt she had to drive her to Clapham instead of letting her go by herself on the bus. Mum said she felt guilty about not taking her gran more often, but, you know, if you don't even remember the dead person, it's hard to visit the graveyard regularly.

"Anyway, they got there, and bought some flowers at the gates, and the old lady filled a plastic bottle with water from a tap. Mum carried the things and held her gran's arm, and they walked to the grave. And then Mum gave the flowers to her gran, who knelt down by the grave. She was—you know—taking out last week's flowers and arranging the new ones in the vase with the fresh water, and suddenly Mum saw someone standing beside her."

Omri sat rigid. He felt as if ice water were trickling down his spine. He could see it in his mind's eye. He saw the whole scene as if it were being enacted in front of him. He even *saw who his mum had seen,* before his father went on.

"She could see her clearly. A woman in an old-fashioned long dress with her hair piled up on her head. There was a strong breeze blowing, but the woman's hair didn't stir. She was looking straight at Mum."

Omri wanted to ask his dad to go on, but he felt frozen, frozen in the scene. He hardly needed to ask. He *saw*.

The woman was Jessica Charlotte.

She took a step forward, nearer to the grave, looking all the time at the young girl standing on the other side of it. She put her hand—it was wearing a long black glove—on the shoulder of the bent old woman, busy with the flowers, who didn't seem to notice. She patted her gently. She smiled a sad, sad smile at the young girl who was going to be Omri's mother. And she nodded tenderly down at the old lady, as if to say, *See how old she is. You must take care of* her *now*. Maybe she even did say it. And then suddenly she wasn't there anymore.

Omri's father was talking. He was describing the scene just as Omri saw it in his head. Which came first—what Omri saw or what his dad said?

When his dad finished, there was a silence, and then Omri said in a choked voice, "Mum must have felt awful."

"About seeing the ghost?"

"No! About all the times she hadn't taken her gran to the cemetery. About the ghost needing to come and—and remind her to take care of Maria."

"Do you think the ghost—was Jessica Charlotte?"

"Of course it was," said Omri simply.

"You sound sure."

"I am."

"Omri—how can you *know* that?"

"Well, it's not because I'm magic. It's just—I've got a very good imagination, and sometimes it just tells me things."

His father looked at him, and Omri heard what he had just said, heard it as his father must have: as proof that Omri had a bit of Jessica Charlotte's gift.

*   *   *

They talked it all over very carefully before anyone else in the house woke up. The sun was well clear of "Peacock Hill" and streaming into the room before they heard the others beginning to stir and had to stop.

Omri—though of course he wanted to see Jessica Charlotte again and thought it very probable that she would have the ability to make them another magic key, one that would work in the car—was very doubtful just the same about his dad's plan.

There was nothing in the Account about her making a second time journey. The first one—when she'd visited Omri and Patrick and sung them a music-hall song—was hinted at in her diary, but nothing after that. Surely if she had been "brought" a second time, and asked to make another key, she would have remembered it, especially so close after the first time.

Omri's father was very interested in the time question.

"Does it work the same at both ends?"

"Yes."

"That's to say, if a week has passed here, a week has passed for the people in the past."

"That's right. I know because when Little Bear came this last time, his baby was about a year old, and it was a year *here* since he was born. Anyway, I knew it before."

"Okay, so let's work it out. How many days is it since Jessica Charlotte came?"

Omri thought about it. A week had passed between seeing her and the day his dad had found the figures and discovered the secret, and three days more had passed since then.

"Ten days."

"Ten days . . ." His dad was looking at the notebook. "So. Right after she came here—no, it wasn't. Let me see. She made the key. That was the day of the parade, the day she said good-bye to Lottie, Armistice Day— November 11th, 1918. The next day she went back to Maria's to 'say good-bye,' pretending she was going abroad. And that was the day she stole the earrings. So that's one day.

"Then, she writes, a week went by. And at the end of that week, she got the news that little Lottie had been accused of stealing the earrings and had run out of the house, and her father, Matthew, ran after her and got run over and killed. And that's where her part of the Account ends."

"Well, there is a bit more . . ."

"Not that you can read. When she got to writing that part, all those years later when she was on her death-bed—" He looked up and looked around. "Maybe in this very room, Omri!"

"No, it was Gillon's room."

"How do you know?"

"I just—" He stopped suddenly. He was beginning to feel creepy about this. He did 'just know,' he was certain. But how?

His father took a deep breath and went on. "Okay. Anyway, when she was trying to write the last of the Account, she became too ill and weak, and had to call in her son, Frederick, to finish it. This last page of her writing—" he pointed to faded, scrawly words that you could hardly make out—"indicate to me that she was not only very ill by the time she came to write it, but that she was writing about a time when she was almost crazy. She felt Matthew had died because of her, that Lottie had been falsely accused, that more terrible things were going to happen because of what she'd done.

"Now, Omri, if you've got a bit of her 'gift,' use it. Imagine her as she was—is—at this moment. Ten days after the theft of the earrings. Three days after she found out about Matthew's death."

Omri didn't have to imagine very hard. He'd been through this already, when he had read this part of the Account. He had almost seemed to be suffering with Jessica Charlotte in this awful crisis in her life. He had felt her guilt, her horror, her remorse. He didn't want to experience that again, or even a shadow of it. It was a terrible thought that, down through the layers of time, she might still be going through that; that if they brought her, they would have to see her going through it.

"She's right in the middle of it, Dad. Her—her—awful time." A new, appalling thought struck him. He took the notebook away from his father and peered closely at the semilegible words. *Alone . . . wandering . . . despair . . . river . . . coward . . . never . . .* He suddenly and shockingly understood the meaning behind the word *river* and the word that followed it.

"Dad! She—she tried to drown herself!"

"What!"

"I'm sure of it! Why didn't I notice before? I was so disappointed that the Account had stopped, thinking I'd never learn the secret of the magic now, I didn't read *into* it like I did the rest. 'Alone—wandering—river—coward.' Don't you see? She was in such a state she wanted to throw herself into the Thames, and maybe she couldn't because she was too afraid. Or maybe she was too much of a coward to go on living. . . . And that's what's going on *right now*, back in her time! Oh, Dad!"

he exclaimed, forgetting to be quiet, staring at his father across the notebook. "We're not going to bring her *now*, are we?"

"If we want her to make us a key, to go back and help Little Bear," said his father slowly, "we'll have to."

4

"River" . . .
"Coward" . . .
"Never"

It was a school day. Omri whispered to his father as the house woke up that he might pretend to be ill so he could stay home and they could talk more. But his dad said no way.

So there was a normal breakfast, and Gillon and Omri set off for school on their bikes. Adiel was having a long weekend "exeat" from his boarding school. Omri envied him. But, no, that was absurd. If he, Omri, were incarcerated in a boarding school, there'd be no question of any adventure.

Actually it turned out that having to be in school was a good thing. It gave his mind a sort of rest. When school was finished, and he went back to thinking about

IT on the bike ride home, he came to it fresh, and at once an interesting thought occurred to him.

Bringing Jessica Charlotte might be a kind of relief to her. She'd enjoyed being with him and Patrick; it had lifted her out of her sorrow about Lottie. Perhaps it would be like that again. However terrible she was feeling, she might feel a little less terrible if she were taken out of her own life and into theirs.

No one was at home when he and Gillon arrived. The door of the cottage was never locked (what a difference from London!), so they let themselves in and made peanut butter sandwiches with milk (their mother had banned fizzy drinks from the house since she went on her health kick). Gillon drifted TV-wards and Omri, seeing him putting down roots at the other end of the house, felt safe in shooting upstairs and fastening the brand-new bolt on the inside of his bedroom door, the one that led to Gillon's room.

He looked at the cupboard.

The mirror in its door reflected his own face back to him. You'd never think it was anything special. Just a little white-painted metal bathroom cabinet, the sort you put medicines and tooth things in. It looked a little smarter since he'd repaired and repainted it, but it was old and essentially commonplace. No one would guess! No one who didn't know would ever guess!

He lifted it onto the floor and opened it. The key was inside. So were the figures of Little Bear, Bright Stars and her baby and the pony, and Matron and Sergeant Fickits. He took them all out and wondered where he could hide them now that the bricks of his makeshift bookshelves had gone. Eventually he found a pretty good place. There was a small, unused, old-fashioned fireplace in one wall. He reached up the chimney and found a sort of little ledge up there. He wrapped the figures individually in Kleenex, put them into a plastic bag, and put this out of sight on the ledge.

Then he wiped the soot off his hands and took Jessica Charlotte's figure out of the cashbox and stood her on the shelf of the cupboard. Just to see how she looked there.

She looked fine, just as he had last seen her, dressed up in her beautiful red dress with the bustle and the big, plumed hat. Her figure was posed in a stagey position, hand on hip, the other hand over her head, waving to them.

Omri stuck the key in the keyhole. Just for somewhere to put it. He wasn't going to do anything, of course—not without his dad.

He closed the cupboard door carefully. There. Now everything was ready. Now he would go and do his homework.

Instead, he turned the key. His hand did it. He couldn't stop it.

It gave him a shock when it happened. He really did try to restrain his hand, but his fingers acted, there was the familiar click, and it was too late.

Galvanized, he turned the key back again and threw the door open.

There she was. But no longer strutting, actresslike, brazen and bold. Now she was lying very still on her face. Her hat was gone. She was in a different dress. It looked strange, somehow. So did her hair. Omri reached in and lightly touched her with the tip of one finger.

She was soaking wet.

All the muscles in Omri's face went slack. He picked her limp wet body up and laid her face up on the palm of his hand. Her face was gray. Her hair and dress streamed with water.

He realized then why his fingers had turned the key when he hadn't meant them to. His fingers knew what they had to do. They had to bring Jessica Charlotte, now. Right now. They had to recall her from the river.

For a split second, looking at her putty-colored face, her closed eyes, her streaming hair, he thought she was drowned. But he knew she couldn't be—she had the rest of her life to live. Still, he had to help her, and there was only one way.

He laid her carefully on his bed, rushed to the fire-place, fished the bag he'd just put away out of the chimney, and frantically unwrapped the figures till he came to Matron. He thrust her into the cupboard and locked her in.

When he re-opened the door, she was standing with her arms akimbo, looking extremely severe.

"My dear young man," she said, "this cannot, I repeat *cannot,* keep occurring. You are going to get me the sack. I had a *great* deal of explaining to do, the last time. Don't you realize there's a war on? These little excursions are all very fine, but we are rushed off our feet. Do you understand? I am *on duty!*"

"Matron! Please! I'm sorry. I need you."

"And the unhappy victims of the Luftwaffe do *not?*"

"Just for five minutes! You must!"

He didn't give her a chance to argue, but picked her up by the waist and airlifted her to the bed where Jessica Charlotte was lying, a waterstain spreading over the quilt. Matron bent over her for only a moment.

"Put her on something firm," she ordered.

Omri transferred them both to his desk.

"Turn her on her stomach."

Omri obeyed. Matron knelt beside the prone figure and began artificial respiration, her hands on either side of Jessica Charlotte's rib cage, rocking to and fro with a strong, purposeful rhythm. After a short time that seemed long to Omri, he heard a sound like a tiny cough, then a choking, then some gasps and groans. Matron sat back on her heels.

"There we are. She'll be all right now. Keep her well covered. You need to get those wet clothes off. . . . Oh. No, I quite see that that would be, er . . . difficult. . . . All right. Go away and get me something to wrap her in."

Omri stumbled to his chest of drawers, got out a pair of woollen socks and some scissors, and hacked out a little blanket. He returned to the desk with his eyes averted and handed it to Matron.

"All right. She's decent."

He looked. Jessica Charlotte's wet clothes had all been pulled off and were lying in a soggy heap. There seemed to be quite a lot of them. Matron was just finishing rolling her patient in the sock blanket like a cocoon. Only her head stuck out.

"Pillow!"

Pillow! Omri's brain raced. A much-folded Kleenex was all he could think of. At least it would soak up the water from her hair.

"There now. She'll do. She's half awake. Something hot to drink, with a drop of Scotch in it. How did this happen? No, don't tell me. I've seen it all before. Very little of that in wartime, y'know. Funny thing."

"Very little of what?"

"Suicides. Too much else to think of. And then, when someone else is trying to kill you, you don't do it for them. Well! I'm off. Have to pass this little lapse off somehow at St. Thomas's. How long have I been, ten minutes?" She looked at an all but invisible watch, pinned to the front of her uniform. "Less. Well, even matrons have to spend a penny occasionally. . . . Hurry up, young man!"

"I can't thank you enough, Matron—"

"Oh, pish, tush, and likewise pooh!"

He dispatched her through the cupboard, and hurried back to Jessica Charlotte. As always when involved in this business, he was beginning to feel frantic and to wish he'd never started. He always forgot this feeling in between.

She was stirring, trying to sit up. He lifted her tenderly back onto the softness of the bed, keeping his hand behind her to support her. "Miss Driscoll?" he said softly. "Are you okay?"

"Why am I—tied up?" she gasped in a panicky voice.

"You're not tied up, you're wrapped up to keep you warm. You—you've been in the river."

She stared up at him. With her hair straggling round her white face and her bare shoulders rising from the blanket that she was clutching, she looked like pictures he'd seen of mad people in old asylums, where they used to take their clothes away and just give them blankets.

"The river!" she cried out suddenly. Then the glassy look left her eyes, and she buried her face in the blanket and began to sob.

Omri found this hard to bear. He crouched beside her till his face was level.

"Miss Driscoll," he said softly, "please don't be upset. It wasn't your fault. It wasn't your fault!"

Her head snapped up. She faced front, clutching the blanket, shivering all over. She spoke sharply between chattering teeth.

"I'm dead. That's what it is. I died in the river and this is my hell. It's only what I deserve."

"No! No! You're okay, you're alive, you're just—just visiting the future like you did before. And you don't deserve to go to hell or to feel so bad. Please don't feel so bad. Honestly, you couldn't help it!"

"I'm a thief and a murderer. I killed my own sister's husband."

"No you did not!" Omri almost shouted. "It was an accident!"

"I caused it."

"You couldn't know!"

Abruptly she turned her ravaged face to him.

"But you! You knew. You could have warned me! You could have stopped me!"

"No, I couldn't—"

"Yes! You said you could see my future. You must have known, you must have done!"

"I couldn't change what happened," mumbled Omri. "It's—not allowed."

She gave him that mad look again, out of the corners of her eyes. "Are you God?" she asked in a small, suddenly childish voice.

"Of course I'm not. I'm Lottie's grandson."

"Lottie's—"

She sat perfectly still. He could almost see her mind working.

"Move back."

He knew why she said that. She couldn't see him properly this close. He moved halfway across the room.

"You're nothing like Lottie. You look a little like me."

"Well, you are my great-great-aunt."

"Lottie's—grandson—"

She couldn't seem to take it in. But then she began to cry again, only not as before. She almost seemed to be crying with joy.

"She lives! My Lottie lives to grow up, and marry, and have children, and be happy! At least I haven't destroyed *her!*"

"Of course not," said Omri, creeping close again. His heart felt monstrously heavy with the truth he couldn't tell her. Lottie lived and grew up and married, sure enough. But when she was barely thirty-one—still in Jessica Charlotte's lifetime—her life was cruelly cut short by a bomb. *The Luftwaffe,* Omri thought suddenly. *The German air force.* In Matron's time, right now, it might be happening. Layers. Layers of time . . . He shivered all over, just as Jessica Charlotte had.

She stopped crying abruptly. She picked up the "pillow" and pressed it to her tiny face to stem her tears and wipe them. Then she put it down and stood up clumsily because of the blanket.

"Where are my clothes? I hope *you* didn't take them off!" she said, with something of her old spirit.

"No, don't worry—a nurse did it. They're here. I'll put them on the radiator to dry them."

"Radiator? Is that some heating device?"

"Yes. They're so small, they'll dry in no time."

He lifted the little pile of wet clothes and squeezed some drops of water out between finger and thumb. Then he began to separate them. Some of the underclothes were so small he could hardly handle them, and he was afraid of them getting lost. He laid his big comb across the ridged top of the radiator and very carefully laid the clothes on top of it—the dress, a black one; an underskirt; a strange, corsetlike thing; some long pantaloons; two black threads that were her stockings. Her shoes were so tiny he had to pick them up by pressing his finger to their wetness. There was also a tiny triangular thing—a shawl perhaps. He unfolded it with infinite care. It was about half an inch square.

When he'd finished he went back to her.

"Miss Driscoll—"

"You had better call me Aunt Jessie."

He felt a strange glow of happiness when she said that. "Aunt Jessie, then. The nurse said you should have a hot drink with whiskey."

"Pray don't trouble yourself. I don't drink spirits these days."

"I—I want to ask you a big favor."

"Ask."

"You know the—the key you made."

"Oh . . . !" she said on a groan. "Don't remind me!"

"I want you to make me another."

"What for?"

"The key you made . . . Look. Here it is." He showed it to her.

She looked at it. "Why is it so big?"

"That's hard to explain. The fact is, you're small."

She was watching him carefully.

"It's all to do with your gift," he went on, "the magic you put in the key."

"Ah. I knew there was something."

"And I need—I really need—another key with the same magic in it."

"You want me to pour the lead for a second key?"

"Yes."

She shrank into the blanket, as if she were deep in thought. Then she straightened and looked Omri in the face. "To do a favor for Lottie's kin," she said, "that would give me something to live for. Give me the key you wish me to copy." And she sat down and began to twist up her straggling hair.

5

Mission Accepted

Racing downstairs to fetch the key, Omri stopped dead.

His parents were out. That must mean in the car. No doubt they'd gone shopping in the village.

His heart was beating at twice its normal speed. He decided he had to calm down. Think. There must be a spare key somewhere, but he had no idea where. No, he'd have to wait—preferably patiently—till his parents returned.

Meanwhile, he would get Jessica Charlotte a hot drink.

He went to the kitchen, built out at the back of the longhouse. It was quite a simple kitchen, with a big oil-burning range which was always warm, day and night. There was invariably a big heavy kettle simmering away at the back of it.

He rummaged in a drawer till he found what he was looking for—a tin of oil; his mum could not abide a squeaking hinge. It had a narrow spout with a little cap on top. He took this off, put it in a sieve, and poured the very hot water over it to clean it. He sniffed it— okay, no oily smell. Then he made a mug of tea with a teabag, added milk and sugar, stirred vigorously, and was just carrying it toward the stairs when Gillon came strolling through from the TV room.

"I see you got your cupboard out of the bank," he remarked.

Omri spilt some tea. "When did you see it?"

"Yesterday."

"Do you have to peep into my room?"

"You have to crash *right through* my room, about fifty times a day. *I* don't get much privacy."

"You wanted the outside room."

"Yeah, I know. I'm beginning to think I messed up there. You've got the best room."

"Yours is bigger."

"This is a crazy old house, no corridors," said Gillon. "You having hot chocolate? You might've made me some."

"Tea," said Omri reluctantly. Gillon knew he hated tea.

Gillon gave him a comic look of puzzlement. Omri turned, anxious to get away, and started up the stairs. Gillon followed.

"About the cupboard."

"What about it?"

"Why'd you get it out of the bank?"

"You told me that it was silly to ask them to take care of it."

"You didn't get it out because of me," said Gillon shrewdly.

"I wanted to have it back," said Omri. They were in

Gillon's room by now. Omri walked straight across to his own door.

"Can I come and look at it?"

Omri turned sharply, nearly spilling the tea again.

"Gilly, listen. I'm not just being—I mean, I'm busy with something. It's something I'm—busy with. Of my own. You can see the cupboard later. D'you mind?"

Gillon looked at him for a moment, then turned away.

"Why should I mind," he said flatly. "I don't care a toss about your old cupboard." It was obvious his feelings were hurt, even though Omri had tried to be as tactful as possible.

"Sorry, Gilly," Omri mumbled, and went into his room. He didn't want to bolt the door because Gillon would hear, and maybe be more hurt. But the need to be safe was paramount. He put the tea down on the desk, and moved the bolt with infinite slowness. Of course it had to squeak.

"Don't worry!" Gillon called through the door. "You couldn't pay me to come in now."

"Sorry," was all Omri could think of to reply.

He hurried to the bed. He was going to have to whisper—no, *breathe*—everything he said to Jessica Charlotte. These walls were thin.

She was there, as he'd left her, in the blanket. She'd twisted up her hair somehow and was looking a little better. He poured a drop of the hot tea into the oil-tin cap (spilling more on the floor than went in) and handed it to her. She took it in both shaking hands and drank and drank. Then she said, "Thank you. Are my clothes dry?"

Omri rubbed the tiny dress between finger and thumb. It *was* nearly dry. He smoothed its skirt with his fingers, held it by its top, and flapped it a little in the warm air above the radiator. He had to stop at once because the flapping nearly blew her drawers away! He handed the dress to her.

"What do you think? Is it dry enough?" he whispered.

"It will do quite well. Please bring my—other garments." He lifted his comb, taking great care to keep it level, and carried it to her. She snatched the drawers and the corset thing and hid them in the blanket.

"I'll go away while you dress, if you like."

"I would be obliged."

He stood with his back to her at the window. For the first time, he stopped to think that his dad was going to be *well* disappointed about his bringing Jessica Charlotte without him.

After a few minutes, she said, "I am ready."

He turned. She was standing on the bed fully dressed. Her little weight made a dimple in the quilt. "Now, where is this key you spoke of?"

"I can't give it to you until my dad gets here."

"Your father!"

"He knows about the magic. He's—"

Suddenly he heard the sound he'd been listening for. The car! He heard it come along the lane and stop near their gate.

"Wait! I'll get it for you!" Omri said, forgetting to whisper, and dashed to the door. He stopped. No, he must go out the other way, through his parents' and Adiel's rooms, and down the other stairs. He couldn't risk leaving the door between his and Gillon's rooms open, especially as Gillon might have heard him speak. He wouldn't blame him if he had a peep now.

He dashed down the other way, out of the house, and

met his parents at the gate. They were unloading shopping from the car trunk.

"Hi, Om. You look as if you've been running!" said his father cheerfully.

"Dad—please—can you come? *Bring the key.*" The last three words were not spoken aloud. He just mouthed them behind his mother's back and gestured turning a key in case his dad hadn't caught on.

Excitement and secrecy brightened his father's face. He hefted a big box of shopping and almost ran after Omri up the path and into the kitchen from the back. "What's up?" he asked eagerly.

"I brought her! Jessica Charlotte!" His dad gasped. "Dad, it just happened, and it's good it did! She was in the river—she was drowning! The magic just got her out in time—I—I sort of saved her life!"

"Is she here?" Omri nodded. "She's upstairs—Jessica Charlotte—she's upstairs now?" his dad said dazedly.

"Yes, Dad! And she's agreed to do the key for us. Only I didn't have it. Bring it up. You can meet her! Come on!"

His father dropped the box on the table with a thump and was halfway up the nearest stairs before Omri could stop him.

"The other stairs, Dad!" he whispered, and pointed upward to Gillon's room.

Down, through four rooms, and up the far staircase they ran, and in five seconds they were in Omri's room. Omri pointed silently. His father followed his finger and turned to face the bed. His face when he saw the tiny figure of Jessica Charlotte was a study in wonder. Omri thought that for him, it was like looking at a famous person, from history or fable, standing alive before him, staring back at him.

He moved toward her slowly. He crouched down beside the bed and smiled at her like someone dazed by a miracle.

"I'm so pleased to meet you," he breathed.

"Dad! Shhhh! Let's go next door!" Omri mouthed.

He picked Jessica Charlotte up very carefully and they went into the parents' bedroom. There his father indicated his mother's dressing-table. It was her favorite piece of furniture. It had a glass top, under which she had arranged a number of family snapshots. Omri put Jessica Charlotte down on this glass surface.

It seemed she could no more take her eyes off Omri's dad than he could take his from her. Her tiny but compelling voice piped, "Are you my Lottie's son?"

"No," said Omri's father. "My wife is Lottie's daughter."

"What is her name—her first name?"

"Jane."

There was a silence. "Well," she said at last. "At least the initial is the same. It is a sort of bond, even if . . . accidental."

"But her second name is Charlotte."

After a beat, Jessica Charlotte said hoarsely, "After her mother?"

"No. After you."

Jessica Charlotte seemed to sway where she stood.

"How—do—you—know—that?" she asked as if she could barely get the words out.

"Because her grandmother told me so."

Omri hardly believed what he was hearing. Was his father making this up? But no. He wouldn't do that. Why had Omri *never* thought to ask if his mother had a middle name? Why had it never occurred to him that his dad must have met Maria?

"Her grandmother!" Jessica Charlotte gasped. "She was my sister."

"Yes. And I knew her. Of course I thought the same as you did—that Lottie had named my wife after herself. But one day before we were married, when I was visiting Granny Marie—"

"Granny Marie!"

"Yes, that's what my wife called her. She got annoyed with my wife over some little thing and said, quite sharply, 'That's your namesake coming out in you!' My wife said, 'Do you mean Mummy?' meaning Lottie, and Maria said, quite tartly, 'Don't run away with the idea that your mother christened you after *herself!* She never thought of herself as a Charlotte—it was always Lottie. She named you after my wick—'" He caught himself and stopped, and then went on "'after my sister, Jessica Charlotte.'"

"Is this the truth?"

"Yes, it is. I remembered it very clearly when I was reading—"

Omri trod heavily on his foot and he stopped.

"Tell me!" she cried, and Omri saw her clasp her hands at her breast. "Is my Lottie still alive?"

Omri's mouth went abruptly dry. He almost pushed in front of his father. "Aunt Jessie, we can't talk anymore. It's—it's not allowed. If we give you the key, can you take it back with you and copy it?"

She switched her gaze to him. He thought he saw a look of eagerness—a sort of blaze—in her eyes. "I will."

Omri put out his hand for the key, and when his father gave it to him, laid it on the glass at Jessica Charlotte's feet. She bent down and looked at it.

"How can I manage to carry something so large and

heavy? I have a long walk home from the Embankment."

"When you get back, you'll be full-size, and the key will be very small. Do you think you can do it?"

"I'll try. How shall I—go back?"

"The same way you came—through Frederick's cupboard."

"Frederick's cupboard? What do you mean?"

"Never mind. It's all in your future. When do you think the key will be ready?"

"Tomorrow."

"We'll bring you back then."

Jessica Charlotte bent down again and grasped the key, holding it below the bulging plastic top part. Just as she was lifting it, with some difficulty, she stopped and pointed at the glass at her feet.

"These are photographs," she said. "Who are they?"

"People in our family."

"Who is that?"

She was pointing to a black and white snapshot of a young woman holding a baby in her arms. Beside her was a tall, good-looking man in naval uniform.

"That's your Lottie," said Omri's father very quietly. "With her husband and Jane. My Jane. Jane Charlotte."

Omri's Aunt Jessie stood with the heavy key, its tip still resting on the glass, in her hands, staring and staring down at the faded photo. When she had looked her fill, she turned, lifted the key, which was nearly as big as herself, and turned her face to them. The tears in her eyes caught the light in star-like pinpoints.

"I will never despair again," she said. "Now please. Send me about my business."

6

Little Bear's Need

Neither Omri nor his father slept much that night. In fact, in the middle of it Omri heard his dad come creaking through the dividing door into his room in his pyjamas. Omri immediately shot up in bed.

"Oh—you're awake, too!"

"Yes."

His father sat down on the edge of his bed. "D'you think she's doing it right this minute?" he whispered.

"Making the key? I expect she's done it by now."

His father shivered a little. "This is so exciting! Listen, I was thinking. If we're really going back to Little Bear's time, we'll need something of his to take with us."

"Yeah . . . that's right."

"Have you anything?"

"No."

"Then won't we have to—to bring him back, just for a few minutes, to give us something of his?"

Omri was glad of the darkness. It hid the grin he couldn't suppress at the boyish eagerness in his dad's voice. It occurred to him that where this business was concerned, *he* was the grown-up, in a way, because he'd had more experience. His dad acted just the way he had, in the beginning. As if it were all a marvelous game. Omri knew better, but his dad would have to learn for himself.

"You're right, Dad."

"Could we—could we do it now?" He was obviously dying to work the magic again.

"Okay!"

There was no moon, and they couldn't see much by the little starlight that came through the small window with its deep-thatched eaves. They couldn't turn a light on for fear his mum would see it reflected through her window. Omri got his flashlight out from under his pillow and switched it on, got out of bed, and went to the fireplace. He reached up into the sooty darkness and fished the plastic bag down.

"Great hiding place!" whispered his father.

Omri took Little Bear's figure out by the light of the torch. He opened the cupboard. There on the shelf stood the plastic figure of "Aunt Jessie" clutching the key. Omri picked it up. He was amazed to see that the whole key, not just the bit at the top, was made of plastic now.

"Look, Dad! This means it's definitely gone back. I wasn't absolutely sure it would, being made of metal—the cupboard's never worked except with plastic. P'raps the plastic part worked for the whole thing—it couldn't just *half* go back."

His father took the figure from him. "How strange!

It's joined to her. It's part of Jessica Charlotte's figure—you can't separate them."

"Come on—let's bring Little Bear back!" Omri stood him carefully on the shelf and closed the door.

"Can—may I turn the key?" asked his dad eagerly.

"Sure, go ahead, Dad."

He turned it. There was a brief, breath-held pause. Then he turned it back, opened the door cautiously, and Omri shone the finger of light directly onto Little Bear. He was standing, arms slightly away from his sides, legs bent, as if he'd just landed from a jump.

He straightened up and shielded his eyes against the bright light.

"Om-ri?" came his gruff voice. He said Omri's name as if it were two words.

"Yes. Are you okay, Little Bear?"

"I am o-kay. You are o-kay? Why sun so strong I see nothing?"

"It's night. We have this special kind of light."

"Take from eyes. It make me like night mouse."

Omri swiftly redirected the beam downward.

"Better! You and father come now with me to my longhouse?"

"We can't come yet, Little Bear. We have to make arrangements. We can't leave just like that."

Little Bear became thunderous. "You have small understanding! Trouble swallows the days. All ask chiefs for wise words, to conquer fear. What can Little Bear tell them? Our land drinks our blood season by season in English wars, now King George says he has no more need of the Six Nations. English change their faces, break their word, let rebels take our land. Now we fight tribe against tribe instead of together as white enemies grow greater."

"The French?"

"No! When Little Bear was young warrior, he fought the French. French lay down guns, go back to France. But now white enemy does not fight and then go back across the sea. Now they stay, move against Indians like wolf packs, more and more. Much trouble. We must travel together, now. We must sit in council."

"Little Bear," said Omri's father, "how will it be, in your place? What will people think when they see us?"

"They will not see. Your people here see me, see wife, see Boone? Not see because we are small here. Easy to hide. When you come to me, you small, too." He looked up at them triumphantly. "O-kay? Little Bear understands magic right?"

"Yes," said Omri. "But, Little Bear, listen. When you come here, you—you bring a sort of toy to life. Last time I went, I was part of a picture on a tepee. I couldn't move or speak or anything. You'll have to have something ready for us to—to bring to life. We won't be much use to you if we can't talk or move."

Little Bear looked thoughtful. "Toy," he said slowly, "what is 'toy'?"

"Something kids play with."

" 'Kids'?"

"Children."

"Ah! We have toys. Small Indian and animal made from corn, animal skin, part of tree. Wife makes good, makes for son and others. I tell her, make toy like you. You come, bring alive."

"We need something of yours, to help us come to you," Omri said. "Can you give us something? Anything."

Little Bear, after a hesitation, slowly took off his belt. "Wampum," he said, "worth much. You take care, give back." He laid it across Omri's outstretched hand. Omri shone the flashlight on it. It was white with tiny purple marks. Omri knew about wampum—what he was look-ing at was shells strung together. But wampum was more valuable to the Indians than mere money.

"I'll take great care of it, Little Bear, don't worry!"

"Now send me back. Bright Stars will make toys. You come soon. Little Bear will wait. Wait *hard*." He put out his hand, and Omri touched it with his finger. "Brother. My heart has trust, you will come to our help," he said gruffly.

When he'd gone, Omri and his father examined the belt under a magnifying glass. Omri explained about wampum, how it was the Indians' money and how the patterns also recorded their history because they had no written language. "And look! See those few purple shells among the white, made into a pattern? Those are the most valuable ones! I bet only Little Bear has a belt with those in, because he's a chief."

"I'll take care of that," said his father. He found a scrap of paper and wrapped the belt in it carefully, put-ting it away in his pyjama pocket. After a moment of stillness, he suddenly said, "Omri."

"What?"

"Did you—did you exactly realize we were going to be *small* when we got there?"

"Of course, Dad! Didn't you?"

"No. And I didn't realize I was going to inhabit a corn dolly, either." Omri gave a snort of laughter, but his father wasn't laughing. After a moment Omri felt his hand grasped in the darkness.

"You're not scared, are you, Dad?"

"Bloody scared," his father replied. "Suddenly."

Things got tricky the next day.

First of all, of course, there was school—and no get-ting out of it—and Omri's dad had things to do.

A man arrived early to pump out their septic tank. They had one because the cottage wasn't on mains drainage. It was a large tank buried in the garden, with a flower bed on top of it, into which all the wastewater from the house flowed. His dad had explained to them solemnly that there were little bugs—bacteria—living in there that devoured any "nasty solids," reducing them to sludge, while liquids soaked away into the surrounding earth. The boys all thought this was hilarious, in a disgusting sort of way.

Anyway, the sludge had to be pumped out every so often, and today the man came to do it, with a vast tanker truck that stood in the lane while something like a giant hose was poked through the hedge, across the lawn, and down into the tank through a manhole. The tanker was pumping away with a loud roaring noise while their father and mother stood watching, when Gillon and Omri set off for school on their bikes.

Omri felt a renewed sense of guilt for making Gillon feel left out the day before, so he decided to chat as they rode along. It took an effort, because he would rather have stayed silent, dreaming and planning and trying to imagine ahead.

"Did you do anything about the camping trip?" he asked.

"Sure," shouted back Gillon, who was slightly ahead, flying along between the high Dorset hedges. "I got the mag after school yesterday and I've been making a list of—" His voice faded as he sailed round a corner, in the middle of the lane.

The next second there was the screech of brakes and that unmistakable metallic clashing sound of a bicycle coming to grief.

Omri automatically swerved in tighter to the edge of

the narrow lane, partly lost control, and bumped up
onto the grass verge just as a red postal van appeared,
almost up on the opposite verge as if it had just nar-
rowly missed someone coming to meet it. Which it had.

The van halted, nearly standing on its bonnet, and
the postman jumped out and ran back around the bend.
Omri, meanwhile, had fallen off his own bike straight
into the ditch that ran alongside the hedge.

He lay stunned for a second, feeling ditchwater soaking his side. His leg had hit something sharp. Then he
heaved himself out the only way he could, by clutching
a handful of stinging nettles in preference to a handful
of hawthorne. He was covered with mud, stings, and
scratches but he didn't notice. He stumbled along the
rough verge round the bend, terrified of what he might
see.

What he saw was the postman, hauling Gillon, likewise muddy and scratched, none too gently out of the
same ditch ten yards farther along. The bike was lying
at a strange angle with its front wheel in the air.

Seeing he was all right, the postman began giving
him what-for in his strong Dorset accent.

"Ye girt young fooil, what ye be thinkin' yer doin'?
Near made me ticker conk out, sno! Lucky me brakes
be sharp—ye'd have bin a gonner! All right, are ye?
Nothin' broke?" He looked as if he might start feeling
Gillon's arms and legs. He was fairly dithering with
shock.

Gillon looked shaken, too. Omri struggled up to him
on wobbly legs.

"You okay?"

"Yeah, I think so. Sorry," he said to the postman.

"Girt young fooil!" he said again, and took himself
off, muttering.

Omri and Gillon looked at each other. Then they burst out laughing.

"You should see yourself!"

"What d'you think *you* look like?"

"Someone who just fell into a ditch?"

They collapsed on the grass, helpless. After a while Gillon sat up.

"You realize we're late."

"We can't go to school like this anyway. We'd better go home and get cleaned up."

"Mum'll have kittens."

They rose slowly and went to their bikes. When straightened out, these proved to be more resilient than their owners. They rode back to the cottage, unfortunately meeting the postal van coming back the other way. The postman scowled out of the window at them, put on speed, and, accidentally or otherwise, sent a shower from a convenient puddle to add a little something to their appearance.

Their mother was waiting at the gate. The postman must have told her what had happened. She grabbed Gillon.

"Are you hurt?"

"No."

"There are times," she said between her teeth, "when I could wish the days of *serious* clips round the ear were not past. You have been told *ten thousand times* to keep in to the side. No, not a word. Get indoors and clean yourself up. Don't imagine for one moment you're getting off school."

"Mum, if we go in now we'll get detention!"

"Just see if I care. *And why aren't you wearing your helmet?*"

Gillon fled. She turned her attention to Omri.

"What happened to *you?* Did you jump into the ditch to show solidarity?"

Omri was beginning to feel the stings on his hand, and various other aches and pains apart from the scratches, rather painfully.

"I think I've hurt my leg, Mum," he said pitifully.

She looked at it. Through the crust of mud it was bleeding in three places.

"All right. Come on, I'll look at it. Put your bike away."

"Does that mean I don't have to go to school?"

"Maybe after lunch."

When Gillon found out that he had to go straight to school and Omri didn't, he naturally set up a howl of protest.

"At least I was knocked off my bike, practically! Omri just fell off! It's not fair!"

But their mother was not to be moved. As soon as Gillon was ready, she clapped his helmet on his head and banished him. Meanwhile she had washed and bandaged Omri's cuts and told him to go and rest in his room while she phoned the school.

Omri only noticed then that the tanker was gone. It hadn't passed them so it must have gone farther up the lane to pump the neighbors' sludge. Omri wondered where his dad had gone when it left. In the same moment that he wondered, the obvious answer came to him.

He remembered in a flash an occasion in the old house, when he'd left Patrick alone with the cupboard. Despite his bad leg, Omri took the stairs two at a time.

He knew exactly where his dad was.

7

A Bitter Disappointment

Omri burst into his bedroom. Sure enough, there was his dad. He had his back to him, blocking the cupboard, and he appeared to be concentrating on something in his hand.

When he heard Omri come in, he turned. His face was pale, and a look almost of anguish was on it.

"Dad! What on earth's wrong?"

Without a word, his father held out his hand to Omri, palm up. As Omri walked toward him, he noticed the cupboard door was open. Jessica Charlotte's figure was standing on the shelf. But it was different. The key was no longer in her arms.

"Dad! You brought her! Where's the new key?"

"Here it is," said his dad in an odd, flat voice.

Omri looked into his hand. It was completely empty.

"Where is it?"

"It's there. Jessie assured me, it's there. She put it

into my hand. She could see it, apparently, but I can't. It's too small."

Omri stared at him, open-mouthed. "Too small to *see?*"

"We didn't think it out properly, Om. When she got back, the key was miniaturized. Right? It would have been very small compared to her, because everything that goes through the cupboard gets small. She said she had a terrible time trying to copy it. When she poured the lead into the tiny mold she'd made she couldn't be sure it would take such a small impression. She was absolutely *bent* on doing her best for us, and she worked 'like a jeweler,' she said, using a magnifying glass and a tiny watchmaker's tweezers and file that she bought specially.

"But of course what none of us stopped to realize was that the *copy* came from her time. So when it came forward to us, when she brought it just now, *it got smaller still*. Now it's a miniature of a miniature. Does that make sense?"

Omri was totally confounded. Of course it made sense. It was obvious. But what a shock—what a disappointment! The key they'd been counting on! Invisible to the naked eye, and completely useless.

His father was showing him his other hand. In that lay the original car key that they'd sent back, full size, part metal, part plastic.

"The original key became big again when I brought her, so big it tore free of her pocket and fell onto the floor of the cupboard." He put it into his pocket.

Omri sat down sharply at his desk. There was a long silence.

"I am so *stupid!*" he suddenly shouted.

"Shhh! No, you're not—"

"Why didn't I *think? Of course* the copy would be small. Smaller than small. She made it. It had to get smaller still when she brought it back through the cupboard."

"That's it, then," said his dad dully. "That's it. That was our last hope."

Omri looked at Jessica Charlotte's figure. He picked it up.

"Did she say anything else?"

"Not much. She said she couldn't stay long. She just said she was glad to have met me. She tried to save face, telling me how hard she'd tried, but I think she sort of realized she'd failed us. She said, 'I fear it won't be any use. I did my utmost, but my gift can't overcome the problem of proportion.' I think I thanked her . . . I know she thanked *me*." After a moment he added, "She sent you her love. She said she wished she'd had a son like you."

"We won't see her again," said Omri sadly.

"No. But there's one good thing. She won't try to kill herself again. It'll be terribly hard for her. But at least she knows Lottie grew up and had a baby."

"Good she doesn't know she died so young."

"She found that out at the end of her life, when she poured the lead to tell her own future. It was in the Account."

They were silent.

"So we can't go, then," said Omri hopelessly.

"It doesn't look like it."

"What about Little Bear? Maybe we could give him some advice from here."

His father frowned. "I'm not so sure we should give him any. Who are we to give the Indians advice? It's like the missionaries, who told them what to believe, and rubbished their religion, destroying everything that had ever held them together."

"But Little Bear asked. Because he guesses we know how things are going to turn out."

His father said nothing. After a while, Omri felt the need to comfort him. If he himself felt this disappointed, he could only guess how his dad must be feeling.

"Well, we could always go camping properly," he said.

His father snorted. "A wet tent on Dartmoor! Fat comfort!" he said violently.

For the next two weeks, Omri had a lesson.

He didn't realize it straight away. But what gradually dawned on him, watching his father, was that he had been wrong and smug to think for one single moment that he, Omri, was the grown-up one here. Being grown up was *attitude,* not experience. His dad proved that *he* was the grown-up.

Omri, for his part, fell into a steep depression. He couldn't be bothered with anything. He did no work at school except what he was forced to. He was rude to his mother. He had a fight with Gillon. He excused himself to himself by thinking that he was desperately worried about Little Bear; but what he was really doing was giving way to a terrible mood, because they couldn't go, because their adventure was canceled.

But his dad was quite different. You'd never have thought he'd had a bitter disappointment.

He carried on just as usual, and was his usual self. He didn't appear to be particularly moody or sad. He didn't say a word more on the subject to Omri. The only way Omri knew he was still thinking about it was that he began to sketch Indians.

A pile of books appeared in the end room, the one at

Omri's and Gillon's end of the house, the TV-free zone. Omri saw this one day when he was passing through from the stairs to the dining room. He paused to look. They were from the London Library, which sent out books to members. They were all about Indians. Some of them were illustrated. It was from these pictures that his dad was sketching.

But he wasn't working much in his studio, which was highly unusual. He spent most of his free time in the end room, reading.

Omri sensed he didn't want to be disturbed or questioned. But he couldn't help himself. After a few more days, he just had to ask. He felt so bad, and it seemed his dad didn't.

"Dad?"

"Hm?" said his dad, from the depths of a book called *The Ambiguous Iroquois*.

"What's the point?"

His dad understood at once, and looked up at him.

"The point, bub," he said, "is to learn all I can."

"But now we can't *go*—"

"I know. It's tough. But I just feel I—owe it to him, somehow."

Omri edged closer. "What have you found out?"

His father closed the book on his finger and leant his head back against the chair. "It's a damn shame Little Bear didn't belong to one of the tribes farther west. Of course in the long term they were no better off, but the crunch hadn't come for them in Little Bear's time. There were still plenty of Indians living their lives in the old way, all across the American West, and that went on for decades, till 'the West was won,' as the old movies say.

"But in the East things were different, and worse, because that's where the first settlers from Europe

66 • Lynne Reid Banks

landed. It was where the French and English wars happened, which the eastern tribes were involved in. By Little Bear's era the settlers were really spreading out and the tribes were being driven away. Some were in danger of being wiped out."

"Not the Iroquois!" exclaimed Omri in a shocked voice.

"How much have *you* read about the Six Nations?"

"A lot."

"So you know that they had a seriously democratic type of government."

"Oh, yes! Some people say the government of the United States was based on it."

"Well . . . I'm not so sure about that. But they made a confederacy with other tribes that were related to them, in order to have peace and to cooperate with each other. They had laws and customs that, in some ways, were better than what white people had. The white settlers called them savages, but by the end of the eighteenth century the boot was on the other foot."

"They used to be terribly cruel," Omri said doubtfully. "The Indians I read—"

"Yes. Many of the tribes were cruel—they were very fierce and warlike. The Iroquois had a fearsome reputation. But according to the accounts of the few unprejudiced white men who traveled among them, they could show us a few things about civilized behavior. Listen to this. I must just read you this—it really struck me."

He put his book down and picked up another called *North American Indians*. It had a number of slips of paper in it, marking particular places.

"The man who wrote this, George Catlin, was an artist. How I'd love to think that if I'd lived then, I'd have done what he did! In the eighteen thirties he traveled and lived among the tribes in the West, the ones who were still living as they always had, who hadn't yet been shoved around and missionized and corrupted by the whites. But of course Catlin knew they were going to be. He'd seen what happened to the ones in the East. This whole book he wrote is full of sadness because he knew that the people he was painting the portraits of, and making friends with, were on the edge of extinction. He used words about them like 'noble,' 'honorable,' 'gentlemanly.' And 'religious'—their own religion, not the priests'. He liked and admired them in a lot of ways, but he didn't like everything about them.

"Once, he had this conversation with a chief of the Sioux. He was saying how bad it was, the way they tortured their prisoners, and when he'd finished some pretty outspoken criticism, the chief mentioned that he'd heard that white people choked wrongdoers to death like dogs on the end of a rope—not enemies but their own people. And Catlin said yes. And did they shut each other up in prisons for most of their lives, sometimes because *they couldn't pay money?* So Catlin said yes to that, too.

"Then the chief said that he'd visited white men's forts and seen soldiers taken out and whipped almost to death, and heard that they let themselves be treated like that by their own comrades just to earn a soldier's pay. And could it be true that white people hit their own children? Catlin had to say they often did.

"And the chief just kept quietly asking about other white people's customs, such as robbing graves and abusing their own women, and Catlin kept making notes and keeping his head down and feeling more and more uncomfortable, and at last the chief asked if it was true that the Great Spirit of the white people was the child of a white woman and that white people had killed him—referring to Jesus, of course. When Catlin had to say yes to that, the chief simply couldn't believe it, and said: 'The Indians' Great Spirit got no mother—the Indians no kill him, he never die.'

"At that point, Catlin writes, he was 'quite glad to close my note-book, and quietly to escape from the throng that had collected around me, and saying (though to myself and silently) that these and an hundred other vices belong to the civilized world. Who then are the 'cruel and relentless savages'?"

Omri took the book out of his father's hands and leafed through it, looking at the pictures, which had all been painted by the author. They were beautiful and striking. Omri was struck by how different the Indians looked from one another, how differently they dressed. Some of them looked almost Chinese. Others looked quite European. This surprised him. He'd always somehow thought about Indians as being all more or less like Little Bear.

"Are there any portraits of Iroquois?"

"Page three seventy-seven," said his dad, consulting a notepad.

Omri turned to that page and saw a picture of a man called Not-o-way, chief of the Iroquois. He was magnificent, with a burst of mixed feathers on his head, a beautiful tunic, buckskin leggings and moccasins, a blanket over his left shoulder, ornamental armbands and belt, and a tomahawk in his right hand. Omri stared at him, playing with the wonderful notion that he might, just might, be Tall Bear's son. Little Bear's grandson.

He glanced at the opposite page and read that George Catlin had admired Not-a-way—"an excellent man"—and learnt from him that the Iroquois had conquered "nearly all the world: but the Great Spirit being of-

fended at the great slaughters by his favorite ꜱ
resolved to punish them; and he sent a dreadful dꜱ
amongst them, that carried most of them off, and ꜱ
rest were killed by their enemies."

Omri's heart sickened. "Weren't there any Iroquois
left at all?"

"That was what Catlin thought," said his dad. "He
was very doomful about the outlook for all the Indian
tribes, that was partly why he wanted to paint them
before it was too late. But they weren't all wiped out,
not a bit of it, so don't despair. And," he added under
his breath, "I don't want Little Bear to despair, either,
however bad things look."

" 'His favorite people,' " said Omri slowly. "The Iroquois thought they were the Great Spirit's favorite
people."

"Yeah," said his father quietly. "The Chosen. Where
have we heard *that* before?"

Omri put the book down. "Have you found out if it's
true, what Little Bear said? Were the English being
rotten?"

His dad was silent for a moment. "You know, Om, we
British were top dogs in the world for quite a long time,
but top dogs often think that power is enough, and that
hanging on to power is more important than behaving
well. We haven't as much to be ashamed of as a lot of
colonial powers, but that doesn't mean we haven't *anything* to blush for. Have you ever heard the expression
'Perfidious Albion'?"

"No? What does it mean?"

"Well, *Albion* was an old word for England, and *perfidious* of course means *treacherous*. In two words, it
means promise breakers, double-dealers. Englishmen
always prided themselves on being men of their word,

but our rulers haven't always lived up to that. I'm sorry to say that our treatment of the Indian tribes that helped Britain in its colonial wars was not a shining example of honor."

"So we kind of owe them."

"Yes. We left our Indian allies in the lurch all right, round about 1783. But there were still decisions for the Indians to take, bad ones that led to extinction and not so bad ones that led to survival, at least for some. You don't know how badly I wanted to find a way to help Little Bear to make the right one."

8

A Different Tribe

The following weekend was fixed on for the preliminary camping trip.

There was no reason at all, now, why Gillon should be excluded, and Omri had the decency, through his bad mood, to be glad of that, anyway. It would have been necessary, but mean, to scheme to keep Gillon at home if they'd been—*going*.

So their mother packed them all sorts of food and drink, and they put the old tent and their grotty old school-trip sleeping bags (their dad borrowed Adiel's) into the trunk of the Ford. They put on ratty clothes and piled washing things and spare sneakers and underclothes and sweaters ready to stuff into a big rucksack their mother promised to produce from somewhere.

And produce it she did—triumphantly, shaking the dust and spiders of ages off it in the yard. A huge, heavy thing adorned with numerous pockets, buckles, and cracked leather straps.

"It's been among my family stuff for years. I found all sorts of strange things in it—an old solar topee and some really lovely old stuff from India."

Omri fingered it. It was very old indeed, and looked as if it must be about to fall apart, but when he tested it by pulling hard on the straps, nothing gave.

"They made them to last in those days," his mum said approvingly.

"What's a solar topee?"

"A pith helmet." Omri looked blank. "I'll show you—follow me!"

Omri gave the knapsack to Gillon—who stood in the yard with it dangling from his hands, as if Omri had dumped a dead dog in his arms, staring at it with incredulous disgust—and followed her into the big barn that had once been used for pigs. A room at the end was filled with his mum's "family stuff." She picked up an old cotton bag and lifted out of it one of those thick sun-stopping hats that explorers in the tropics used to wear. It, like the knapsack, looked old and none too clean—it even had some spots of paint on the brim—but still usable.

"It must have been your grandfather's," Omri said.

"Matt's. Yes, it was. All the stuff from India is his." She picked up a strange thing like five upside-down bowls made of bronze, engraved with dragons, with a cord going through the middle of them. Attached by a rotting piece of string was a stick. His mother held them up and struck them one by one. They made a pleasant bell-like sound, each a little higher than the last, till the smallest bowl at the bottom made a final musical *ping*.

"Why don't you hang that indoors, Mum? It's nice."

"Okay! I'd forgotten I even had it till I looked inside the knapsack."

"Was there anything else in there?"

"Yes, quite a lot. It's all wrapped up. But I opened this—look."

She took some yellowing tissue paper off a tiny statuette of a black elephant about two inches high.

"Ebony," she said, "with ivory tusks. Isn't he sweet? Here, you have him."

"Thanks, Mum!" Omri took it from her and put it into his pocket, thinking he would stand it on one of the shelves in his room. "Did you know you had all this?"

"Well, yes and no. I remember some of it. Granny Marie used to let me play with some of these things when I was a little girl. There were more elephants then—they stood in a line on the mantelpiece, biggest first, smallest last. Maybe they're all here somewhere! I really must go through all this stuff one day. . . . And this gong thing hung in the hall, and everyone who came to the house wanted to have a go with it. You'd hear it chiming faintly and know that someone who'd slipped out of the room had sneaked into the hall to try it out. Only very old and stuffy people resisted. . . . Granny used to call it her young-at-heart chimes."

The weather was quite warm for October, but on Dartmoor it might well be different—you never knew. "Very bleak, Dartmoor," said their dad. They managed to fit all their extra clothes except rubber boots and anoraks into the big knapsack. Gillon thought it was revolting and said he'd be ashamed to be seen with it. "If *only* we'd had time to order some new stuff! Oh well, when we do the real trip, with Ad, we'll have a decent nylon one. Let's go somewhere where there's nobody but us,

Dad. They'll think we're paupers or something, carrying a lump of old junk like this around!"

Nevertheless, he put the knapsack on the backseat, which he'd "bagged" because he always fell asleep on car journeys, and despite his disgust, he wanted to use it to lean against. That suited Omri, who far preferred to sit up front.

At long last—it was nearly noon by the time they were finally ready—their mother kissed them all through the various windows, and then ran off because she thought she heard the phone ringing from across the lane.

"Ready, boys? Right. We're off."

And their dad put the key in the ignition and switched on the engine.

The next moment, Omri wasn't in the car anymore.

He had the most extraordinary jigging, jumping sensation. He seemed to be being pulled from his head, from his hands—even his feet were being lifted and dropped to a strange rhythm. He was dancing! But not of his own free will. Someone, or something, was *making* him dance.

His eyes, which a moment before had been looking through the windscreen of the car into the deeply shadowed back of the parking bay, were suddenly blinded by bright light so that he screwed them shut. But his body kept up this senseless rhythm, his arms and legs flying, his head bobbing.

And now he could hear noises. Squawking music like a tinny horn, loud, strange voices, but most clearly of all—a drumbeat, quite close to him. It was drumming out the rhythm he was dancing to.

He was terribly shocked and frightened. But he had

to see what was happening. He opened his squeezed-shut eyes a crack—and then wider.

An amazing scene met his eyes.

He was out in the open air—hot air, blazing with sunlight. Before him was a colorful crowd of people—women, men, children—most of them staring at him. They were brown people with black hair. Many of the men wore white turbans and baggy clothes. The women wore—

The women wore saris.

Omri knew a sari when he saw one. They brought just one word into his addled, aching head: *India.*

India. Indians. What had happened? Could the magic make a mistake like a person—take him back to *the wrong Indians?* The notion was so bizarre that if he hadn't been so completely shocked and scared, he would have burst out laughing.

The thought only lasted a nanosecond, and after that for a while his brain simply refused to function. All he knew was that he mustn't show these staring people that he was alive. The forcible pulling and dropping of his limbs and head went on to the throbbing of the drum and the tootling of the music. He let himself stay limp and just tried to orient himself.

Something kept moving and dangling in front of him. He saw it was strings—two of them. He followed them downward with his eyes and saw that they were attached to the cloth above his knees. It was these strings that were pulling his legs up in the dance. As his knees were lifted up, he saw that his legs were covered in bags of bright purple silk.

He swiveled his eyes to the side, and thought he heard a surprised gasp from the people who were grouped in front, watching. He turned his head a little to the left. His arm was in a sleeve, a full sleeve of red and gold material. There was a string around his wrist that kept up a steady pulling and releasing to make his arm move.

He felt his head jerked till it faced forward. Then he felt himself being moved from the spot—he was being made to dance to the left—then back to the right. He could have resisted, but he dared not. Because he knew, now, not only where he was, but what he was.

He was a marionette. He'd brought a string puppet to life!

But how? . . . How? . . . Jerking on the ends of the strings, his head on fire with pain, he tried to think, but it didn't make any sense!

Even when he had been part of Little Bear's tepee and the Algonquin warriors had been attacking the village and threatening to set the tepee on fire, Omri had not been more frightened than he was now. At least then he had had some vague idea of what was happening and where he was. He'd known that Boone and Bright Stars were somewhere close at hand. He'd known that Patrick was at the other end, that he knew what to do, that he could bring him back if only he turned the key in time.

But this was different. This was a trip he hadn't planned or prepared himself for. Besides, he was in pain. The string for his head was fixed to his hair. Every time that string was jerked, pain ran all over his head so that he wanted to shout out.

But he mustn't!

He did the only thing he could. Apart from holding his head up, he went limp and let the puppet master dance him around. His thoughts were fuzzy with fear. He mustn't give himself away—that was all he knew.

That one eye movement had nearly done it. Some in the audience had noticed that he'd turned his eyes like someone alive. He stared to the front and let his body be jiggled and jerked and just let the fear wash through him.

The music ended. The strings made him fall forward into a bow. The audience clapped and shouted. The head string agonizingly pulled him upright. And then he saw somebody pushing through the crowd, coming to stand in front of the low wooden stage. A big, smiling white man in a khaki safari suit with—with a—what was it called?—a solar topee on his head.

He said something in a language Omri couldn't understand. It was something approving, praising. Then he put out his hands and took the strings above Omri's head away from the puppeteer. There was a lot of laughter and interest in the crowd, which was gathering around now. Some dark-skinned little boys wearing only white cloths wrapped around their hips and legs were trying to touch Omri and stroke him, but the big man held him high, out of reach of their hands, and laughed, and seemed to tell them not to touch.

Omri had to force his eyes to stay wide open. But as soon as he was above the eye level of the children he was able to blink and close them for a moment against the glare and the frizzling heat.

He heard the clink of money. He risked a quick peep. He saw what must be the puppeteer, a big man in a turban in bright, showman's clothes, bowing and smiling through his black beard. A huge hand came and fondled Omri, and the man said some words that Omri guessed were some kind of fond farewell. He realized that he had been sold to the white man in the solar topee.

The solar topee . . .

As the white man moved away, still holding Omri up by the strings, high above the heads of the children who followed, laughing and reaching up their hands to touch and grab him, he was dangling just level with the big man's head. The solar topee had a mark on the top of its brim that he recognized. He had seen it, only a short while before—just before he had been dragged back through time. White dots, as if some small spots of paint had fallen on it.

And then he knew who this white man, who had bought him from the puppet master, was.

It was Matt. His own great-grandfather.

9

In the Bungalow

The little crowd of children followed, shouting and jostling, for a long way through the hot, noisy, exotic streets. Matt got tired of holding Omri-the-puppet high above his head, and handed him to a man walking behind him. He was an Indian—a servant, Omri guessed.

At last the children stopped following and the man lowered his arm and draped Omri by the strings over his shoulder. The pull of the head-string on Omri's hair was simply agonizing, and Omri thought all his hair would be pulled out before they got wherever they were going.

Mercifully, Matt decided to ride rather than walk. He hailed a sort of cart with two wheels and long shafts, but to Omri's amazement, instead of a horse it was pulled by a man in a loincloth and bare feet, who grasped the shafts in either hand and ran along, pulling Matt through the devastating heat. The servant didn't ride—he ran along behind—but Matt wanted to look at his purchase, so he took Omri away from the servant and laid him on the worn leather seat beside him.

The awful pulling on his hair stopped. Omri lay on his face. He felt Matt examining his costume, fingering the silk. It seemed impossible he wouldn't notice that the "doll" inside the costume was warm and alive, but he didn't. *Everything* here was hot, which perhaps explained it.

The rickshaw man ran through more streets and pulled up. Matt picked Omri up—by the waist, fortunately. Omri drooped at both ends. How he wished he were back in his own time, the controller, the one in charge! What on earth was going to happen when Matt inevitably noticed that he was alive? Maybe he'd think there was something devilish about him and destroy him! That would almost certainly happen if an Indian were to discover him. Maybe Matt would take a more rational, less superstitious view. But what was rational about this?

The blazing heat abruptly cooled down as they entered a building. The light became dimmer; the windows were shuttered against the boiling sun. Omri became aware that he was sweating all over. He felt a faint swish of cool air, coming and going, and risked a peep around as he hung upside down. He saw an Indian in a white turban and baggy trousers sitting cross-legged in a corner pulling rhythmically on a rope. Omri saw that the rope led upward to a huge swaying fan near the ceiling.

The next moment everything went wild.

He was flying through the air, and fear shot along his limbs, but the flight was short and he landed softly on a piece of furniture. Matt had tossed him a short distance into a wicker chair. Luckily it had a cushion on it.

Omri heard Matt clap his hands. A servant came in and bowed, and Matt gave him an order which, though it was in English, Omri was too wrought-up to understand. Then Matt slumped into another chair and took off the solar topee. He laid it on his knee and scowled as he examined its brim.

Omri could see him clearly. He was a handsome man, just as Jessica Charlotte had said—tall and straight with thick fair hair, rather a red face, and a blond mustache. He wore a short-sleeved khaki shirt and shorts, knee socks, and lace-up shoes. Despite the heat he looked quite unrumpled, and apart from sweat stains under his arms you would think he had just got dressed.

My great-grandfather, thought Omri wonderingly. His fear lessened a little. He remembered everything Jessica Charlotte had written about how kind and good Matt was. But then she was in love with him. And he hadn't been "good" enough to let her go on seeing Lottie. Omri had decided when he read the Account that his great-grandfather had a hard side to him.

Omri lay very still, just as he had fallen. His arms and legs began to ache from tension. When the servant came back with a small tray on which was a bottle of whiskey and a glass, Matt poured himself what Omri's father would certainly have regarded as a stiff drink, got up with it, and strolled to the other side of the room, where he stood with his back to Omri, fiddling with something. This gave Omri a chance to shift a bit in his sweaty silk clothes. Despite the fan, he was desperately hot.

What was going to happen?

He thought about what *had* happened.

What was the last thing before he had arrived here? They'd been in the car, the three of them, and his father had put the key into the ignition and switched on the engine.

It came upon him with the force of revelation. The little elephant had brought him back! Obviously, the key was magic after all—the original car key that had gone back with Jessica Charlotte. How could this be possible?

Omri racked his brains. When they'd looked at her figure, the key had become part of it, held in her arms—the whole key had become plastic. It had gone back in time with her, as part of her. Could it be that just being, for the journey, part of Jessica Charlotte, had put magic into it—Jessica Charlotte's "gift" magic? Or maybe it was what his father had said—that she had "bent all her efforts" on making the new key—the invisible, useless key—magic. Some of that focusing, that force of her will to satisfy their request, might have spilled onto the original key.

It must have done.

In which case, they—he and his dad—could go back to Little Bear's time after all!

Omri felt his heart leap. It could still happen—their great adventure! *If* Omri could get out of this unplanned, unscheduled, dangerous one.

Wait.

Omri's body must, at this moment, be in the front seat of the Ford, unconscious. Wouldn't his father notice? Wouldn't he guess at once what had happened?

Evidently not, or he would have turned the key and brought Omri back already.

His father must think he'd just fallen asleep.

But after a while—say, a couple of hours, the time it

would take to drive to Dartmoor—surely his dad would begin to wonder why Omri didn't wake up. If he tried to wake him and couldn't, he'd realize then. He would guess, as Omri had, that the key was magic. He would turn it in the ignition and bring him back safe. In fact, as soon as he stopped the car and switched off the engine, it would happen.

Matt turned and came back toward Omri, a small, thin cigar in one hand and his drink in the other. He stood over the chair, looking down at him. Omri, trying to contain his wild trembling, lay as still as he possibly could.

"You're a little beauty," said Matt. "That rogue robbed me blind, but I couldn't resist you. Maria will adore you . . . and Jessie will make you perform, perhaps." He took a sip from his glass and laid it down. "Come on, I'll take you to meet your lady friend."

His *what?*

Matt's hand reached out.

Omri found himself praying that Matt would pick him up by the strings, even though it would hurt. If he picked his body up now, he would surely notice he was not a doll. But just as Matt's hand touched him, someone came into the room, and he turned sharply.

It was another servant, a woman. She wore a plain green sari with the end carried over her head. She put her hands together with the fingertips to her lips and bowed her head submissively.

"Yes, Jothi, what do you want?"

"You sent for my husband, sahib. He sent me in his place."

"He knows he's in trouble!"

"Yes, sahib."

"How could any man be so stupid as to paint a ceiling and not cover everything up underneath? Look at this."

He strode to his original chair and picked up the solar topee.

"Look! Spots of paint! It's ruined. I shall have to get a new one."

"I am truly sorry, sahib. I will try to take paint away. Please, sahib, do not punish my husband. He is not a careless man. He is full of grief that he did this thing." She kept bowing as she spoke, and there were tears in her voice as if she were really frightened.

Omri watched Matt from his prone position on the chair. His face was redder than before, and he kept waving the solar topee angrily.

"Very well, Jothi! You take it and try to get the paint off. Then we'll see." His voice was stern.

The woman bowed deeply, took the solar topee with a quick, nervous movement, and ran out of the room.

Matt strode back to Omri's chair. He scooped up the strings and swung him away from the support. The pain in his head, which he'd expected, didn't come—the head string was left loose and only the ones on his wrists were taut. He hung from his wrists and swung helplessly as Matt carried him briskly from the room, leaving the old man pulling patiently on the fan rope.

Omri let his head hang down and tried to subdue his fear. After a short walk along a corridor, Matt entered another large, shuttered room. It was hotter than the other; there was no fan puller in here. It seemed to be some kind of storeroom. Big tin trunks were stacked against one wall. There were boxes and pieces of furniture and a crude bed made of wood with woven strings for a mattress. Peeping from under his hair, Omri saw something weirdly familiar lying on the bed. It was the big knapsack, only now it was clean and new with all its straps a bright tan color with silver buckles.

Leaning against this in a sitting position was another puppet.

It was a girl puppet, Omri noticed, with flowing jewel-colored clothes and glittering mock jewelry. Her hair was hidden under a bright blue scarf with a silvery border. She had gold shoes with turned-up toes. Her strings were arranged carefully above her, over the top of the knapsack.

It wasn't till he was level with her that Omri noticed something utterly unbelievable.

He got such a shock that he made a sound, but fortunately Matt was coughing over his cheroot and didn't hear it. He sat Omri down beside the girl puppet and carefully draped his strings over the top of the knapsack so they wouldn't get tangled.

"There," he said waggishly. "You two are a pair. Sweethearts, eh? A gift for my sweetheart. Be good now!"

And he turned and walked out, leaving a fragrant trail of cheroot smoke behind him.

Omri waited till the door closed. Then he looked again at the girl puppet at his side.

The girl puppet at the same moment turned her head toward him. They stared at each other.

She had Gillon's face.

10

The Girl Who Was Gillon

If Omri had for one moment expected to see Gillon, staring at him from under a girl puppet's head scarf— if he had stopped for a second to think it possible that his brother might have "come back" with the knapsack he was leaning on in the car—he would have expected him to be looking totally terrified. Baffled. Gobsmacked.

But he wasn't. His eyes were narrowed, his mouth was tight, and his expression was one of pure, unadulterated fury.

"I knew it," he ground out between clenched teeth. "I knew you were behind this somehow."

Omri's mouth dropped open.

"I've been sitting here," Gillon continued, "in this ridiculous girlie gear, just waiting for you to turn up to laugh your arse off. Do you know how hard it was, just getting those stupid strings unknotted? Did you have to get one tangled up in my bloody *hair?* You know what,

I have *always* known there was something really spooky going on with you. Don't think you had me fooled. So go on, surprise me—how did you do it? Hypnosis, that's it, isn't it—you've been secretly studying hypnotism. Or it's something to do with that cupboard. I just knew you'd use it to play some stinking trick on me one day! Well, don't just sit there! If you could see yourself! Get those stupid strings off—you look a total dork in those harem pants and that fancy blouse! No, don't say it, I know I look even more daft, dressed up in a skirt, or whatever this—this *thing* is—"

"It's a sari," croaked Omri. "It's—it's very pretty. You—you look—a real dish—"

He dissolved into hysterical laughter, tried to stand up, tripped over his leg strings, and fell over on the rope bed so hard he got his head stuck in one of the gaps.

"Oh no—pull me up—" he choked, trying to free himself and getting more and more helplessly enmeshed. "I'm stuck!"

Gillon stood up on the ropes, grabbed Omri by his head string, and yanked him ungently free. He clearly did not share the joke.

"When I wake up from my trance," he said grimly, "or whatever, I am going to make sure your buns get stuck in the nearest barbed-wire *fence*. Now jack it in and tell me what you're playing at and how you pulled this off!"

Omri lay back, hiccuping. He wrenched the strings off his wrists and knees and struggled with the one tangled in his hair. He tried really hard to get control, but every time he looked up through his tears at Gillon, standing there in his glamorous Indian getup with a face of thunder under the silver-bordered head scarf, he had to stifle explosions of mirth.

At last Gillon gave him a sharp kick in the rear with his turned-up-toed shoe. As he did so, his other foot slipped through a hole in the mattress and he dropped through like the demon king in a pantomime. Omri became completely helpless, wheezing and choking with laughter.

"Stop it, you idiot," Gillon hissed, trying to haul himself out. "Where are we and where's Dad and what's the story?"

Omri heaved himself upright as well as he could, and gave Gillon a hand. "Well. It's not a trick. I can't explain it all now, but the fact is, we're back in the past. That man who brought me in is our great-grandfather, Mum's granddad. We're in India."

"India. Granddad. The past. Of course, I should have guessed," said Gillon sarcastically. He looked down at himself. "And is it really me inside this—this fancy dress? I mean, I haven't turned into a girl, have I?"

Omri could feel the hysterics coming back. "Maybe you'd better check," he wheezed.

Gillon checked, and breathed a sigh of relief. "So why am I dressed like one?"

"That doll was probably the only toy near at hand when you got here," Omri said.

"You are being *really helpful*. Exactly how did I 'get here'?"

"The knapsack brought you."

"The knapsack. I'm trying so hard not to kill you. All right. I bite. How did the knapsack 'bring' me?"

"You were touching it in the car when Dad turned the key. It was the key that was magic."

At this point, Gillon lost it completely. "Magic! Are you mad! Don't tell me you believe in magic!"

Omri felt exasperated at such obtuseness. "Gilly, look

around you. This is real. We've traveled through time. We're small—we've brought two puppets to life. Of course it's magic. Just get your mind around it."

Gillon face sagged. He stared at him. Then he sat down rather suddenly on the ropes. His feet dangled through two holes and he clutched a strand of rope with each hand. He seemed to need to hold on to something.

"You've accepted that you're now a puppet nine inches high," said Omri quietly. "Is it so much harder to accept magic?"

Gillon said, after a bit, in quite a different voice, "I'm scared. Om—I'm so scared."

"Don't be—it doesn't help."

"We really are small, aren't we? I mean look at this bed, it's like a football field with holes. And that man! Blimey, I just closed my eyes when he came in. I didn't look properly, I didn't let myself. A *giant* . . . a giant great-grandfather . . ." His face crumpled. Gillon, who Omri hadn't seen cry since he was about eight.

Omri crawled over to him across the ropes. He put his arm around his brother's shoulders.

"Don't, it's okay, Dad'll bring us back, we're quite safe," he said, with a confidence he didn't completely feel.

"Safe! What if the giant notices we're real? What if anybody does?"

"They won't hurt us."

"You're kidding! It'll be like Pinocchio and Stromboli!"

"This is a storeroom. Nobody probably comes in here. We'll be left in peace in here until Dad—"

To give the lie to this comforting assurance, the door to the room opened and two children came in. Omri twisted his head and gave them one terrified look. They were like the ones in the square who had tried to touch and handle him.

"Flop!" muttered Omri, and flopped. After a stunned second, Gillon did the same, but it was too late.

The children had *seen*.

Unfortunately Omri had flopped with his head turned away, so he had to use his ears to determine what was happening. There was an excited buzz of whispering. He heard the faint sound of small bare feet crossing the floor. Then he sensed something warm hanging over him, hesitating—a hand. It touched him, felt him, turned him over. He almost fainted from the feeling of powerlessness. All the defense he could think of was to freeze, to stretch his eyes, trying to look like a painted puppet. But it was useless.

Two pairs of sharp young eyes were examining him from about a foot away. They were much wider open than his own. A brown, grubby finger poked his cheek and his stomach and was snatched away. The children—a boy and a girl—looked at each other. The boy said something. Then he reached over and gingerly picked up Gillon.

Gillon didn't bother about trying to look like a puppet. He sprang to life in the boy's hand, struggling, clawing, and kicking. The boy held on, until Gillon, turning his head, bit his hand. At that, the boy dropped him back on the bed and jumped backward with a yell. Gillon bounced once and then struggled to crawl away.

The girl, who only looked about six, ran to the door with her hands over her ears, uttering a wail of fear. The boy sprang after her, slammed the door shut, grabbed the girl, and gave her a good shake. Then he took her by the arm and dragged her back to the bed, telling her off all the way. Omri could well imagine what he was saying—"Don't make a noise, stupid, someone'll come! Let's find out about this for ourselves!" Just what anyone would say, anyone with a bit of sense.

An argument ensued, which the boy, who was a few years older than his little sister, won. Meanwhile Omri and Gillon were as far away as they could get on the mattress, pressed against the wall, clinging to each other. Omri managed to whisper to Gillon, "It's okay, they'll probably just play with us. Don't fight them! Don't frighten them!"

"*Me* frighten *them!*" said Gillon between chattering teeth.

The boy let go of the girl and squared up to Gillon. He said something to him—a question. Of course, in Hindi. But it was strange. Omri could guess what he was saying, because this, or something very like it, had once happened to him.

"He's saying, 'Let me pick you up,'" he said to Gillon.

"How do you know?"

"Well, wouldn't you? Nod to him, but tell him to be gentle."

Gillon threw him a look. But then he nodded to the boy and put his hands out in front of him, palms down, and made a "gently" gesture. His hands were shaking.

The boy reached out carefully, ready to snatch back his hand if Gillon turned fierce again. He put it round Gillon's waist. He lifted him very slowly until Gillon's face was level with his.

Gillon pushed the head scarf off his head and said in a deep voice, "Hallo. I'm a boy. A guy. A bloke." He showed off his biceps, but unfortunately the Indian boy thought he was threatening him and thrust him, suddenly and sickeningly, away from him to arm's length.

"It's all right!" called Omri. "He just wants you to know he's a—a sahib!"

The two children looked at him swiftly.

"Sahib?" said the boy, and looked back at Gillon. "Memsahib."

Omri shook his head hard. "No. Sahib."

The boy scowled under his black brows. He seemed to make up his mind, and handed Gillon abruptly to his sister. She nearly dropped him, but he snapped an order at her. She looked at him fearfully, then looked at Gillon. Her face softened. She squeezed him, giggled, and, climbing onto the bed, sat cross-legged and began to take Gillon's clothes off.

"NO! NO! Stop it—you can't—I'm a fellow, I tell you, let me alone!" shouted Gillon at the top of his very small lungs. He twisted and jerked and fought, but it was no use.

The girl took the end of the sari in her right hand and flicked Gillon away from her. He rolled off the edge of the bed and fell to the floor, the long piece of silk unwinding swiftly, somewhat breaking his fall. She twitched it to free the last bit, leaving Gillon flat on his back in a little red blouse, his Turkish slippers, and nothing else at all other than a tape tied tightly around his waist.

He clutched himself modestly and drew up his knees.

"This is the worst," he muttered furiously. But it wasn't, because the boy now picked him up and gazed at him in astonishment. The girl too.

Then they both looked at Omri.

"Memsahib?" the girl asked.

"No, no! I'm a sahib, too!" Omri hastened to say, repeating the biceps gesture. "Boy, like you!" He pointed.

"Not like you," he added, shaking his head and pointing to the girl.

The two children looked at each other and burst out laughing. She picked up the sari and, laying Gillon on one end of it, began rolling him back into it. She had barely finished carefully tucking it into the waist tape when suddenly there came the sound of an adult voice, calling. Probably, thought Omri, it was Jothi, the servant woman he had seen before.

Both the children jumped guiltily. The boy threw a conspiratorial look at the girl and picked up Omri. Then he said something which was clearly "Come on! Let's get out of here!" He thrust Omri legs first down the front of his loincloth, climbed onto the bed, opened one of the shutters, and the next moment Omri felt himself and his captor dropping through space. A jolt as they landed. A scuffling and more jolts as the boy turned and caught his sister as she let herself fall from the window. Then they were running, running through the heat on hard-packed red earth.

11

The Snake Charmer

As the boy ran, Omri, jolting about, trying to hold himself steady by clutching the roll of cotton at the waist of the loincloth, was trying to figure out *time*.

How long had he been here?

One hour? More? If his body were still in the front seat of the Ford, and if the Ford were rolling along the main road to the southwest on the way to Dartmoor, his dad *must* soon notice that he was not just normally asleep. That Gillon, in the back, slumped against the ancient knapsack, was also unconscious. It wasn't like either of them to sleep through a daytime car journey. Anyway, his dad always stopped off for a coffee and a snack when he was doing a long drive.

It couldn't be much longer before they were taken back. It was just a matter of hanging on.

Unless . . .

Unless Omri's dad had *himself* "gone" somewhere when the key turned!

Did he have anything on him that would take him back to some station in time, some "layer" of the past? Something in his pocket, perhaps, as Omri had had the little elephant?

In which case . . . there would be nobody to turn the key, nobody who *knew* how to bring them back.

Horrendous. The worst . . . Back here in nineteenth-century India for good . . . No. He wouldn't believe anything so appalling. He pushed the thought from his mind.

He craned round the boy's thin waist and looked behind. He could see the little girl panting along in his wake. She was holding Gillon tightly pressed to her chest. Omri could see he was clinging for dear life to her blouse, with his legs scrabbling and swinging about, trying to find purchase on the folds of her skirt.

Where were they going?

They were running past a line of bungalows, set about with palms and other tropical trees. The homes of rich people . . . Omri could see Indian gardeners at work, and in the street was a passing parade of rickshaws, people on bicycles, carts pulled by buffaloes, many people on foot, and an occasional horse-drawn carriage, always occupied by a white person, the men in khaki safari suits and the women dressed much like Jessica Charlotte, only in more summery clothes. The air was hazy, and there was a strong smell of dust and flowers and spicy cooking, mixed with a sharp, acrid choking whiff of burning rubbish. The sun beat down on them. Omri began to wish *he* had a solar topee.

Suddenly they were back where Omri had started—in the big open space. He noticed now there was a market in progress there, but it wasn't like an English one. There was a terrific din, for one thing, and masses of color and movement as hundreds of people struggled to buy and sell in the thick crowds of animals as well as humans.

There were few stalls or tables; mostly people had their wares laid out on the ground: mounds of fruit, fires cooking things, cages with animals and birds in them, sacks full of all kinds of strange things Omri had never seen before—seeds, powders, roots, bunches of greenery, nutlike things, which added a new, intriguing medley of smells that Omri caught and sniffed as his captor ducked and squirmed among the sellers.

At the far end was the stage that Omri had been "dancing" on when he first arrived. It was empty now. The formal entertainment was over, though there were various jugglers, musicians, and magicians moving about the crowd. Omri saw a man up ahead, sitting cross-legged in the dust with a basket in front of him, playing a pipe; a large snake was rearing out of the basket, swaying in a sinister fashion. . . . A cobra! Omri knew it by its hood. The boy was going to pass right by it!

Omri instinctively ducked as they squeezed past. The cobra's head was just level with his face, well within striking distance, but it never even moved—it must be half asleep!

The boy ran up to the stage and took a flying leap onto it, which brought Omri's stomach halfway to his mouth. Immediately, a big man with a beard and a curled mustache leapt on from the other side and ran at him, shouting, threatening him with his fist. The boy promptly jumped down again. At this moment, his little sister came puffing up. They crouched down almost under the stage and held a conference. This gave Omri and Gillon a chance to exchange a few frantic words.

"I told you! Stromboli! They're going to try to earn money with us!" hissed Gillon.

"Yes. And we must just do it. Whatever they want."

"What? Dance? *Sing?*" Gillon was aghast.

"Just jump about! Nobody'll pay any attention, they'll think it's a trick! Look at all the people here who are doing crazy things—"

"You are *nuts*. If this crowd sees two stringless puppets 'jumping about,' they are going to tear us to pieces between them!"

Omri thought fleetingly of the dozens of street urchins who had tried to get their hands on him when they thought he was just a regular puppet. "So what do we do?"

"Lie down and pretend to not be alive."

Omri realized that that was their best bet. Besides, the kids deserved to be shown up. If he had ever tried to put *his* little people on show, it would have served him good and right if they'd lain down and played dead.

The boy raised his head and peeped across the stage. The angry man with the mustache had gone. . . . He and the girl stood up cautiously. The boy took a deep breath and started to shout. He was trying to attract a crowd to watch the "show," but he could hardly be heard, and nobody paid attention. He shouted himself hoarse, and the little girl squeaked and waved her free arm every now and then, the one that was not clutching Gillon. At last it looked as if they would have to give up.

But then, suddenly, a merchant from a nearby stall came to their rescue.

He moved to the children, smiling a broad snowy-white smile through his gray whiskers. He bent down and evidently asked the boy what he was trying to do. The boy, who was nearly in tears, explained, with gestures. He jerked Omri out of the top of his loincloth and held him in front of the man's face and shook him. Omri hung limp. He could just imagine what the boy was saying: "I want people to watch! Look! He's alive!"

The merchant hardly glanced at Omri. He smiled indulgently and patted the boy's head. He said something soothing, and turned back to his stall. He had a real stall with brass and copper pots of all shapes and sizes ranged on it, and others dangling from a rail beneath the awning. He reached between them and unhooked something from deep in the shadows of his stall.

Omri gasped. *It was the chimes*—his mother's "young-at-heart" bowls. Only now they were new and shining reddish bronze in the sun. He could see the beautiful, exotic designs of dragons clearly on the upturned bowl shapes.

The merchant had a stick in his hand. He held up the bowls by their cord and struck the largest one at the top. It issued a deep, resonant, gonglike tone. People nearby stopped what they were doing and glanced round. The merchant, smiling broadly, struck the next bowl, and the next, down to the smallest. Then he played a little tune with the five notes at his disposal. By this time a small crowd had gathered.

The merchant gave the boy a little wink. Then he stepped onto the stage and began to harangue the crowd. He pointed his stick at the two children, and evidently advised people to watch. He made jokes, and people laughed; Omri could see they were getting into a good mood, ready to be entertained. The merchant beat the chimes again, and then reached down and, putting his hand into the boy's armpit, hiked him onto the stage in one easy movement, like an elephant lifting something almost weightless with his trunk.

Next moment Omri felt himself snatched out of the boy's hands. A big, powerful hand held him now and raised him high, shaking him above the crowd, while the resounding voice went on—a skilled showman, this. He had the crowd with him now; scores of people were crowding to the foot of the stage, laughing and excited.

The little girl reached up her hands, one of which held Gillon. The merchant handed his chimes to the boy and took Gillon away from the girl, while eager hands from the front of the crowd lifted her onto the stage beside her brother. Now Gillon, too, was being waggled and dangled before the audience. Omri could easily imagine that the man was saying, "Look! Puppets without strings! Now watch how the little ones will make them dance!"

The big man suddenly decided to get more playful. He tossed Gillon one way, Omri the other! They flew past each other, each suffering an agony of terror before the opposite hand caught each of them. The crowd applauded this little piece of juggling. Encouraged, the man did the same trick several times more. Omri heard Gillon let out a cry as he hurtled past, the kind you make when you're on a terribly scary ride at a fair, but fortunately nobody seemed to hear. Omri, for his part, thought he might very well throw up. What if the man missed, and he dropped to the stage? He could hardly keep still. He wanted to twist himself free, but he knew his only hope was to lie perfectly limp, with tight-shut eyes. It had been Gillon's good advice—Omri only hoped his brother was taking it himself!

He felt himself being passed back to the boy.

The crowd was silent now. You couldn't hear anything

except the cawing of crows and the more distant noises at the far end of the square. It was a poised, anticipating silence, like a held breath.

The boy held Omri up before his own face. The big, dark eyes in the thin brown face stared into his. He could plainly see that Omri was alive, that he was *there*, and he whispered something to him, and again Omri guessed what it probably was: "Go on, do it for us, *please!*" And a ridiculous, quixotic, and terribly dangerous urge came over Omri.

He wanted to do it.

Impressions and ideas flashed through his head. He guessed these kids were the children of Matt's servants. He knew, from the little scene in the bungalow sitting room, that Matt could treat his servants unkindly. Jothi had looked really frightened, as if, were her husband to lose his job because of spilling paint on the solar topee, it would be a complete disaster for them.

The children were thin, like their mother. The reason the boy's eyes were so big was because his face was bony and pinched. The plea in those eyes was plainer than language.

Looking sideways, Omri saw the little girl, smiling, hugging Gillon to her chest like a beloved doll. Like a magic doll who can make wishes come true.

Omri knew it would be far, far safer to pretend they were just toys, and hope no one would notice. Let the kids be shamed, let the crowd jeer at them or even chase or beat them for disappointing the people. Soon, soon, Omri's dad must notice, must stop the car, turn the key, bring them back! And then he and Gillon would be out of it! What did a couple of skinny Indian kids who lived decades ago matter?

The boy squeezed him gently, like a hug of encouragement, and bent down. The next second, Omri's feet were touching the stage.

He did not go limp and fall down. He stood there, swaying.

The crowd gasped.

The merchant began to play a little tune on the chimes. Omri slowly lifted one foot and then the other. He lifted his arms. He turned his head.

He did it all stiffly, like the doll in *Coppélia,* the ballet his mother had taken them all to see once when they still lived in London. Not like a real live person.

The crowd was paralyzed. Omri could see their faces, huge and terrifying, like open-mouthed gigantic masks, all their dark eyes fixed on him.

He let his eyes slide sideways to see what Gillon was doing. He saw him lying on the stage, but his head was up and he was watching him with the same stunned expression as the masklike faces of the crowd.

And suddenly, the merchant looked down and saw them. Really saw them.

He let out a harsh cry. He stopped tapping the chimes and let them fall with a clash. He just stood there. When the music stopped, Omri stopped, one foot and one hand in the air. He didn't know what to do next. There was a terrifying silence.

And then, into that silence, a gentle little thread of music floated. Weird music. Nothing that had happened since they got here had made Omri so sure that he was in another time, and in another dimension of existence, as that sound. It was played on a pipe this time, and Omri saw the crowd part; and the old Indian who had been playing for his snake slipped through, blowing on his pipe.

He squatted down on his haunches till his old, wrin-

kled brown face was level with Omri's. His eyes twin-
kled under the voluminous folds of his white turban,
and something passed from his eyes to Omri's. He didn't
seem at all surprised. He looked at Omri as if he
loved him.

He nodded as he played, as if to say, "I know why
you're doing this. You're a good boy. Go on." And Omri,
as if the music moved his body without his own will,
began to dance again.

It was *beautiful,* what happened to him then. He became a dancer. He had never danced in his life, except
jigging about to pop music, but now he danced, really
danced. He felt no inhibition, no restraint, and his body
behaved as if it had always done this. He lost the stiff-
ness and his movements became more and more free,
more and more in tune with the weird little thread of
music that seemed to weave itself right through him
like his own sinews and command him just as much as
the puppet strings had, two hours before.

At one moment he became aware that he was not
alone, that Gillon was moving about near him, but basically Omri was lost in his own, somehow deeply private,
experience. It was so intense that he lost all fear, all
apprehension of what might result from what he was
doing. He forgot who he was. He swayed, and jumped,
and twisted his arms and hands and feet into strange,
exotic positions. He felt quite crazy with sheer, physical
happiness, as if he had suddenly found he could fly.

And then the music stopped and it was over.

Omri sank down onto the stage, completely exhausted. And things started to hit him.

He came to himself, back to a realization of where he
was and what he was. He was small and surrounded by
giants, and they were all throwing things at him! He

curled up instinctively and covered his head with his arms.

Then the little boy snatched him up and held him, and hugged and kissed him, and the things that were being thrown bounced off the stage and hit the boy's legs and he kept stooping to snatch them up and tuck them into his loincloth, because they were coins. Omri, dazed and bewildered, looking down, saw that other things were landing on the stage, rings, bracelets. . . . There was a deafening noise of applause and shouting.

The little girl was kissing Gillon, kissing her brother, kissing Omri. The big merchant had recovered himself. Though dazed and bewildered, he was embracing the two children by the shoulders, smiling and bowing, taking the credit. He handed the chimes to the boy and bent down and started scooping up the money and jewelry.

At that moment Omri saw Jothi—Matt's servant—forcing her way to the front of the hysterical crowd.

She was crying and tearing her hair. She reached up and grabbed both the children quite roughly and shook them and slapped them both, one with each hand, and then grabbed them again and hauled them off the stage. The boy dropped some of the coins he'd picked up but he held on to the chimes. Jothi flung the girl over her shoulder, holding the boy by the arm, and dragged them both off at full speed through the throng.

And Omri?

Omri felt himself falling. As the boy was pulled off the stage by his angry mother, he dropped him! In the crush and chaos, nobody seemed to notice, and quick as thought Omri rolled into the merciful darkness under the stage.

If he could have seen what was happening to Gillon, he would have had more than himself to worry about.

Gillon was dangling perilously by one leg from the tiny hand of the little girl, who herself was hanging head-down over her mother's back. And as the trio pushed through the crowd, the mother delivered a last exasperated slap on the child's bottom, which loosened her shaky grip on her "doll."

Gillon fell headfirst to the ground.

12

An Iroquois Doll

Omri scarcely had time to draw one dust-choked breath in the darkness under the platform before he felt a sensation of swift, sudden—transference. Not bodily movement—a kind of spinning, whisking feeling, not even of being spun or whisked through air but through some other dimension. At the same time—in that same split second—he was conscious of an overwhelming release of tension.

He was going home. He knew it. It was like no earthly feeling of relief—it was better. He was going back where he belonged, to his own time and his own body.

He lifted his head, opened his eyes, and saw a rooster.

He was looking through the windscreen of the car at the dark back of the parking bay. The rooster was perched on a pile of logs. . . . It was all quite familiar, but he was disoriented for a moment. Then he heard a voice, his mother's voice, almost screaming.

"Lionel! *Lionel!* Wake up, what's wrong, oh do wake up, *please!*"

He felt something bulky stirring on his right side. He turned. His father was there, behind the steering wheel, lifting his head which had been bowed on his chest. His hands moved, flexed, and for a second his father looked at them as if surprised to see them. He looked up at his face in the driving mirror. An expression of incredulous relief came over it. Then he turned to the window on his side.

Omri saw his mother standing there bent over. Her hand was through the open window. She was holding the car key.

With a sudden jerk, Omri looked over his shoulder.

Gillon was there, in the backseat, leaning against the aged knapsack. He wasn't waking up. His hair had blood in it. Blood had made a small runnel down his forehead, across his closed eye, and on down his cheek.

What happened right after that was all confusion for Omri. He felt so tired he could hardly move or think, but around him everything was moving and his parents' voices were echoing and booming through Omri's head as if they were all underwater.

His father stumbled out of the car, clutched his head in both hands, and fell back against the door for a moment before straightening up. His mother was opening the back door, and next minute Gillon was gone, in an upheaval of movement and exclamations. His mother must have handed him to his father, because the next thing Omri knew, his mother had come round to his side of the car, opened the door, and was half helping, half lifting him out. She was almost gibbering.

"Darling! Darling, are you all right? What happened?

I came out to feed the chickens, thinking you were miles on your way to Dartmoor, and found the car still here, the engine running, all of you unconscious. Oh, Omri! My darling, I thought—I thought—" She clutched him tightly in her arms and muttered into his hair, "I thought you were all dead!"

It was just as well she was holding him. His legs were giving way under him. She had to help him back across the yard and the lane, up the path, and into the house.

There was then a timeless, muddled patch when Omri half lay in an armchair in the living room, trying to get his head back together, while a doctor was called for Gillon. By the time he arrived, Gillon had come to. He was lying on a sofa with rugs over him, and his mother washing the blood out of his hair. Omri, as if from far away, heard him moaning and heard his mother urging him not to move, not to try to talk. . . . The doctor examined him and said he seemed all right but he'd have to have a head X ray and could someone drive him to the hospital.

"I will!" said their mother immediately.

The doctor picked Gillon up in his arms, still wrapped in a rug, and went out of the house. Omri's mother, following, stopped beside Omri's chair.

"Omri, will you be okay? Dad's upstairs. I have to drive Gilly to the hospital."

Omri sat up sharply. "In the car? You're going to drive him in our car?"

"Yes . . ."

"Can't the doctor take him?"

"Why?" Her eyes focused on him. "Omri, is there something wrong with the car?"

"No—no—only . . ."

"What?"

"Have you got the car key?"

"Yes—"

He clutched her arm. "Please, Mum. Use the spare."

His mother gave him a funny look, but she went to the little box of hooks by the front door, hung one key up, and took the spare key.

"You rest. I'll be back soon."

As soon as the door closed behind her, Omri leapt out of the chair, fell back into it again, and rose more slowly. Carefully he climbed the stairs and crept into his parents' bedroom. His father was lying on the bed with his shoes on, apparently asleep.

Omri put a hand on his shoulder and shook him gently, then harder.

"Dad! *DAD!* Wake up!" Omri felt scared to death suddenly. But his father stirred, shook his head, sat up, and put his head down between his bent legs. "Are you okay, Dad?"

"I don't know . . ." he said in a hollow voice. "I suppose so. I feel weird . . . utterly weird. . . ."

Omri sat down on the bed. He waited a moment with his heart pounding, and then he found the courage to ask, "Where did *you* go?"

His father raised his head sharply. Omri could see a change in him. He looked suddenly older.

"I went back," he said. "The key—the key worked after all."

"Don't I know it! But where—"

"The belt. I had the wampum belt in my pocket."

"You mean—you went back to Little Bear's time?"

His father nodded.

Omri gazed at him, excitement replacing the fear. Suddenly he reached over and shook his father by both shoulders.

"Well, don't just sit there, Dad! Tell me!"

"Tell me about you first. And Gillon. Gillon went somewhere, too. And he got hurt."

"Yeah . . . that girl—she was holding him upside down—she must've dropped him. . . . Don't worry, though. Jothi was so tiny. . . . Gilly didn't have far to fall. . . ."

"Omri! What are you talking about?"

"Dad, I'll tell you later! *Tell me about you!*"

His father drew a deep breath.

"I don't know if I can describe it."

"Describe what was around you."

"I can't."

"Just anything! What could you see?"

"Nothing. I couldn't see anything."

"What do you mean? Were you blind?"

"Yes. Blind. And I couldn't speak either. I couldn't— breathe."

"*What?*"

He shook his head. His face was white. He swallowed. "I—I kept trying to draw breath in through my nose, through my mouth. I couldn't."

"How could you stay—alive—if you couldn't breathe?"

"Omri, I don't know! But some air must have been reaching my lungs somehow, maybe through my skin, though I wasn't breathing. I can't tell you how terrible it was till I—I realized I wasn't suffocating. Then I sort of—accepted it. And the panic died down a bit. At least, until—"

"Could you hear?"

"Yes, I could hear. I heard all sorts of sounds. Voices. Loud, they seemed to boom, but no clear words."

"They were talking Iroquois, of course!"

"And there were lots of other noises—a fire crackling and insects whirring, buzzing, whining—and dogs—"

Omri thought he would burst with impatience. "Yes, Dad, yes! But just tell me what *happened.*"

His dad drew a deep, shaky breath.

"I'll try. I was lying down. After the first—horror—of not being able to see or speak, of feeling I couldn't breathe, I tried to move, and I found every other part of me—worked. I got up. Of course the first thing I did was put my hands to my face. I got the most ghastly shock. The worst—the worst shock of my life."

"What, Dad? What?"

His father swallowed again and turned stark eyes on him.

"I didn't have a face."

Omri sat in silent horror.

"Nothing. No eyes, no nose, no mouth. A smooth face of skin and bone with—no features."

For Omri, a memory flashed. Stuck to the outside of a tepee, two-dimensional, helpless, dumb . . . a totem animal of some kind but able to see and hear, though not move. But this! This was a thousand times worse!

"Go on. What happened?"

"I just stood there. What could I do? I was in a nightmare. Then I felt something pick me up."

"Was it Little Bear?"

"Yes. Not that I knew it then. I was so afraid! But he held me quite gently and I got some notion of how small I was. There was a pause. I suppose he was looking at me. I put my hands up and pulled them down my—my face. I heard him—give a sort of gasp—an exclamation—like a curse. Then I felt him carry me along. I felt the air of outdoors and heard a whole new lot of sounds. He stopped, and I felt him sort of shaking me, and heard him talking in that strange language. He sounded very upset and angry. Then I heard a woman's voice. She sounded—I don't know. Not exactly apologetic but patiently defending herself. Then he walked with me again, and began to talk English to me."

"What did he say?"

"He asked if I could hear him. I nodded. Then he said he was sorry. Bright Stars had made dolls for us to come into, but they were Iroquois dolls. He said, 'Iroquois make doll without face.'"

"Maybe it's part of the religion. Maybe Bright Stars won't agree to make dolls with faces for us. Dad! I don't want to go back and have no face!"

"I don't want to go again at all. It was—"

He broke off and then just sat still for a while.

"We've been to India," Omri mentioned at last. This extraordinary information, he felt, hardly competed with what his dad had been through.

"*What?*"

"Yes."

"Well? Tell me!"

"Back to my great-grandfather Matt's time. Gillon went, too, because he was leaning against Matt's old knapsack, and that took him back. And we were puppets. But Gillon was a girl puppet."

His father's mouth twitched. "He must've loved that!"

"It seems more—more random when you go back. Because there were no plastic figures then, the magic has to work on whatever there is. Just bung you into *something.*"

"Is Gillon okay?" his father abruptly remembered to ask.

"Mum's taken him to get an X ray, but I think he was just knocked out."

"Tell me about—India."

But Omri said, "It's too long to tell now, Dad. What we have to do is plan. Did Little Bear say anything else?"

"Just that we should hurry up and come properly, both of us. He seemed very disturbed and anxious. He promised there'd be—well, faces, next time."

They looked at each other.

"You didn't mean it, did you, when you said you didn't want to go back?" Omri asked anxiously. "Because we'll have to risk it. We must go back and help him. We absolutely must!"

By the time Omri's mother came back with Gillon, now with a dressing on his head and looking a lot better, they had made a sort of plan. But Gillon was now a major worry.

"We can't take him. We can't possibly take the risk. There won't be a third 'man toy' ready for him."

"But now he's been back once—"

"Maybe he won't remember. Maybe his knock on the head will have made him forget."

It hadn't. But what it had done was to make his adventures in India go rather fuzzy. And as he had had no notion of the magic before it overtook him, he rationalized the whole thing into a dream.

He was full of it. It was he who told the parents the story of the Indian adventure, though in rather garbled form (Omri kept absolutely quiet—it wouldn't do to admit that his dream had agreed with Gillon's), but their mother was too busy fussing about what had happened to put them all to sleep in the car, to take it in. His dad, however, listened in wonder and fascination.

"Isn't that just the weirdest dream you ever heard, Dad!" Gillon said at the end.

"I could tell you a weirder one that I had," said their father, "but you'd think I'd lost my marbles completely."

"Fumes," said their mother shortly.

"What?" they all asked.

"Fumes. Exhaust fumes. It must've been. That's the only possible explanation. There's a leak of some kind, you were all breathing carbon monoxide, and you all passed out and had delirious dreams. And if the car had been in a closed garage, or maybe even if I hadn't come out when I did, you'd probably all have died. *And that car had its service two weeks ago.* Just wait till I get it back to that garage!"

Omri was hugely relieved that she hadn't believed a single word of Gillon's story. He didn't believe it himself. The only thing that seriously bothered her was how Gillon got his head injury. That was one of those little mysteries that was destined never to be solved.

13

The Key Turner

Omri was surprised his mother didn't notice, in the days that followed, that he and his father spent so much private time together. But she was completely fixated on Gillon. After his two recent mishaps, she decided he had become accident-prone and she was afraid to let him out of her sight. So that although in Omri's opinion Gillon had now completely recovered, he was still home from school, being spoilt absolutely rotten and loving it. However, as he kept boring his mother (and anyone else who would listen) by recounting his "dream" over and over again, with embellishments, it seemed probable that her indulgence would soon come to an end.

Meanwhile it was quite useful to have her mind on other things. It left Omri and his dad with time and privacy to plan.

They'd already decided when they would make the trip. There was some kind of teachers' in-training day coming up at the end of October which would close schools on the Monday. So Omri and his dad talked openly at meals about a short camping trip together. There was no question of Gillon going; he didn't even want to. He couldn't explain this, but Omri understood. Even though Gillon thought the India trip had been a dream, nevertheless he'd had his fill of adventure for the moment.

Early on, the idea of Dartmoor was privately abandoned. They decided to go instead to a place nearer home. Omri's dad took to going for long, exploratory walks and drives. At the end of one of them, he was so excited he came to meet Omri on his way home from school.

"Peacock Hill!" Omri's dad said breathlessly. Omri had told him his private name for the hill he could see from his bedroom. "It's perfect! Only two miles away, and once you're up at the top in that little circle of trees, you can't be seen."

"Can you drive up there?"

"Yes, on a cart track. I'd have to back down again, which wouldn't be funny, but it can be done."

"If there's a track, other people must go there."

"Maybe they did once. It's pretty overgrown. I think just the occasional walker goes there now."

But that still left the main problem unsolved. They discussed it endlessly. Who would send them to Little Bear's time? Who would be around to turn the key in the ignition and bring them safely back?

"It must be someone we can trust. Someone who won't ask questions, who'll just walk up there and do it at the time we arrange."

"But there's no one like that! You'd need a robot.

Imagine finding two people unconscious in the car—who wouldn't ask questions?"

"What we really need is someone who already knows."

And then, of course, the solution—blindingly obvious, why hadn't he thought of it sooner?—flashed upon Omri.

"Patrick!"

"Omri," said his dad after a moment, "you are a genius. Write to him immediately, and I'll write to his mother."

Omri didn't stop to think it out. He just rushed upstairs and dashed off a letter to Patrick (who, maddeningly, was not on the phone) at his home in Kent. He wrote "Private and Confidential" on the envelope, and at the start of the letter, he wrote: BURN THIS WHEN READ.

> *Dear Patrick,*
>   *My dad has found out. I didn't tell him, of course. He found out by accident. Don't worry, he won't tell.*
>   *This is to ask you to stay with us like you did before, on the long weekend. You* must *talk your mum into it. Then we're going to a place my dad's found. We'll pretend we're going camping, the three of us. Only we're not really. We're going back to help Little Bear. He's in trouble. We've found a way. It does work, we've proved it. I'll tell you everything when I see you. Say you'll come.*   *Omri.*

Reading this, Omri's dad frowned.

"You don't think you ought to tell him a few more details—such as that he won't be coming with us?"

"Couldn't him and me go first—do part of it together?"

"He and I," grated his dad, as usual. (He was a pro-

noun freak.) "I don't know about that. All I know is that he can't do the main part with us."

"So, basically, we're inviting him to be a sort of gopher."

"No. A key turner."

"What's the difference, Dad?"

"Not much," his dad admitted. "From what I know of Patrick, we're going to have to handle this rather tactfully."

"You mean I am," said Omri glumly. He lost every bit of good feeling he'd had about the coming adventure in bad feeling about exploiting Patrick.

Patrick was on the phone twenty-four hours later to say that he wouldn't miss it for anything on earth.

He arrived by train, unaccompanied, as he had before. This time, as a seasoned traveler, he was rather blasé about the trip.

"Mum'd told the conductor to look after me," he said. "Can you believe she'd do it? Humiliation time! He kept coming round asking if I was all right! I mean, grotesque or what?" After that he talked about nothing but the coming adventure. He thought it was terrific that Omri's dad knew all about it.

"It's really too scary on your own," he said. "I can't wait. I haven't slept since I got your letter. . . ."

Omri and his dad said very little. But Patrick was too excited to notice.

When they got to the cottage and hallos had been said, Patrick dragged Omri to the wild end of the garden for a private conference.

"Look what I brought!" he exclaimed, bringing his closed hand out of his pocket.

Omri guessed what he would see, before Patrick's

opening fingers revealed the figures of Boone the cowboy
and his wife, Ruby Lou. They were sitting on Boone's
black horse, Boone in front, Ruby sitting sideways behind him still in her wedding dress—which, when real,
was of silk and lace ruffles—her veil thrown back, her
red leather boots sticking out incongruously under the
white frill. Boone was bareheaded. They were both smiling their post-wedding smiles of happiness. Boone held
the reins in one hand and something white in the
other—a chunk of wedding cake, halfway to his grinning mouth.

"You're not planning to take Boone and Ruby Lou
back!" said Omri.

"Why not? They belong in the Wild West. They could
help. And they'd go back like Boone did before. I mean
he'd be full-size—he could help us."

"No, it wouldn't work. He was full-size before because
he went back with Bright Stars in the tepee. If he came
back with us, he wouldn't be full-size any more than we
would. Maybe he'd be even smaller, like he is compared
to us, now. *Microscopic.*"

"We could send him back first, with one of the others,
in the plastic tepee, like before. He could be waiting
for us."

"He'd probably be killed by the Indians before we got
there! Imagine it, a white guy not even from their time,
suddenly appearing, on a *horse* which they'd *want,* with
a woman all got up in a wedding dress—"

"They might think she was a goddess!"

"Goddess! Don't be daft! They'd kill Boone and carry
her off. That's what they did with white women in those
days—they carried them off and made them part of
the tribe."

Patrick snorted. "I wouldn't like to be the Indian who tried to carry Ruby off!"

"We can't take risks like that."

"Well, I'll tell you one thing," said Patrick, "I am definitely going to bring them through the cupboard. I have to know how they are. Just for a visit. Omri, come on! You brought yours."

"My dad brought them."

"Yeah. Wow. I have to hear all about that."

So they sat under a tree and Omri began to tell him. Oddly enough, it was the stuff about Jessica Charlotte that Patrick was most excited about.

"The magic pulled her out of the river! But that's weird. How come it happened at just the right moment?"

"I know what my dad thinks," said Omri soberly. "He thinks I've got a bit of magic in me, from Jessica Charlotte, because I'm her posterity."

"Post-what?"

"Descendent, then. Her relative. Dad thinks it can be passed on, like her gift is in her genes."

"She didn't wear jeans!" And Patrick collapsed with laughter and rolled on his back. Omri, feeling the old irritation with Patrick, sat still, frowning. There had always been this side to him. He was a good mate and often had brilliant insights into the magic, but he could be a complete idiot sometimes. Vaguely rude jokes about Jessica Charlotte struck Omri as being completely out of order, especially when he remembered the terrible ordeal she was going through, back in her time, which he couldn't even help with.

"If it hadn't been for her, we wouldn't be able to go at all," he said stiffly.

Patrick glanced at him, saw at once he'd gone too far,

and sat up again. "Sorry," he said. "I was really laughing at the idea of you having magic powers. I wouldn't laugh at *her*." After a moment's thought, he said, "But if you did have some of Jessica Charlotte's gift, wouldn't your mum have it too?"

Omri grunted. He didn't want to tell Patrick about his mother's seeing Jessica Charlotte's ghost when she was young. He thought Patrick just might laugh again. He told about the key and the car. Patrick was absolutely riveted.

"Have you tried it?"

"Yes. We've all been back. Gillon and I went to India, of about eighty years ago I think."

Patrick's jaw dropped. *"Gillon* knows?"

Omri shook his head and told Patrick about his being dropped on his head and thinking he'd dreamt the whole thing. "I'm a bit worried that when he *really* gets his head back together, he'll realize that dreams just aren't like that," he said. "For the moment he hasn't even thought it might have been real. Well, you wouldn't, would you?"

"*I* would," said Patrick. "I'd know it wasn't a dream! Well, go on, tell what happened! India! Blimey! Did you meet a snake charmer?" Patrick did a shimmy with his head and arms.

"As a matter of fact—" began Omri, but just then his mother called them for tea and they had to go back into the house. They didn't get a chance to talk again until they were in bed in Omri's room that night. And that didn't happen until late because they'd had to pack the gear to give the trip the appearance of a genuine camping trip.

Omri tried to tell Patrick about India but they were

both too tired. Besides, Omri was feeling uneasy and guilty about The Plan.

"Patrick," he mumbled as they were both on the brink of sleep.

"Hmph."

"You do realize you can't go back with Dad and me."

There was a longish silence and Omri thought Patrick was asleep. But he sat up abruptly as the penny dropped.

"What do you mean, I can't go back?"

"I mean, for the—the long part of the trip."

"You mean, for the *main* part! The good part!"

Omri was silent.

Patrick got up off his makeshift bed on the floor and switched on the light. His face wore an expression Omri had seen there before, when they'd been younger. It was not an expression that filled him with confidence that Patrick was going to cooperate.

"Let me get this straight. You've brought me all the way here so I can send you and your dad back to Little Bear's time while I—" He stopped. "While I—what, exactly?"

Omri told him The Plan—how he would send them, and then walk down the hill and make an excuse to Omri's mum. "You can say you don't feel well or that we've had a row."

Even as he said it, he heard how terrible it sounded.

"*I* see," said Patrick in a voice dripping with sarcasm. "And then I spend two days here with your *mother* and then do a ten-mile hike back up the hill—"

"Two miles," mumbled Omri.

"Oh, *thanks*. So sorry. Two miles. And turn the key at the right time. And bring you guys back, dead or alive, after you've had the adventure of your lives. And then, if I've been very good, I get to hear all about it. Have I got this right?"

"Er . . . sort of. But—"

But Patrick wasn't listening. He was too mad.

"So I'm just here to be useful. I'm not going back at all. Is that what you think?"

"Oh, of course you're going back! You'll go back with me, first, before me and Dad go for the—the main part."

"For five minutes, till your dad gets fed up and turns the key."

"Er—no—we thought about two hours—"

"Bloody well think again," said Patrick shortly. He switched off the light, and Omri heard a thud as he flung himself down and then a sharp jerk as he pulled up the covers.

Omri's dad's instructions to him, last thing, to "get a good night's sleep" necessarily went out of the window.

14

Patrick's U-turn

Next day, however, it seemed as if it was Patrick who had thought again.

Omri woke from a shallow, dream-fractured sleep expecting a major row with him. But it didn't happen. They got dressed, Patrick avoiding Omri's eyes, and went down to an early breakfast without anything further being said.

After breakfast they loaded up the Cortina. Gillon helped. He seemed to be having some regrets, now, about not coming, but his mother said he wasn't fit enough. She meanwhile was busy in the kitchen preparing enough food to withstand a siege.

"Will we be able to take some of that back with us, Dad?" Omri whispered as they bumped shoulders at the back of the car, loading the tent and the cooler into the hatchback.

"I presume so, if we're touching it," whispered back

his dad. "I'm more concerned about taking useful things like this." He held up a Swiss Army knife with a lot of different blades.

"I wish we had a gun," said Omri. "We might need it."

His father, who was deeply opposed to guns, gave him a look. "Don't be silly. We couldn't even shoot a fly with it, *there*."

"Oh! Of course." Omri shivered slightly.

"Patrick seems very quiet this morning. Did you speak to him?"

"Yes."

"Well?"

"He—he didn't seem too pleased."

"I'm not surprised. But he agreed?"

Omri shrugged. He was bewildered by the change in Patrick this morning. Now he was approaching across the lane, laden with sleeping bags and a small stove.

"Where do you want to stow all this?" he asked flatly.

Omri's dad took it from him and loaded it carefully. "Go on, boys, go and get the rest," he said.

Omri and Patrick walked back to the house together. Omri was dying to speak, to ask, but he didn't know how. This silence between them, after last night, was as suspenseful as a held breath, but Patrick seemed determined not to break it. They made several more journeys to the car with food, blankets, and clothes.

Then, at the last minute, Omri had to dash up to his room because he'd forgotten to pack his pajamas, which of all useless items his mother insisted he take. While he was up there he paused to look at the cupboard.

Perhaps he ought to bring Little Bear back, just for a moment, to warn him they were coming. Make sure the dolls were ready for them. Why hadn't he thought of that?

He hastily took the plastic bag from its hiding place and extracted Little Bear, shut him in the cupboard, and swiftly turned the key. Just as he did so, he became aware of somebody behind him. He swung round, his heart nearly flying out of his mouth. It was Patrick.

"What are you doing?" Patrick asked quietly.

Omri explained quickly. Patrick narrowed his eyes and came closer.

"Go on then. Open the door."

Omri did, and there was Little Bear standing on the shelf. He looked angry, and, ignoring Patrick, burst straight into a stern speech.

"Many days pass! Maybe like other English you forget you gave word!"

"No! We couldn't come just like that, Little Bear. We had to arrange things. We're coming soon, today."

"Our need is great. *You come,*" he said, and it was an order. "More days and it is too late to hold council."

"Are the—the toys ready?"

"Ready many days!"

"How many are there?"

Little Bear held up two fingers.

"What about one for me?" It was Patrick's quiet voice.

"Ah, Pat-rick. You come with Om-ri and father?"

"Maybe," said Patrick steadily.

"No toy ready. Two is enough," said Little Bear, folding his arms.

There was an uncomfortable silence.

"Right," said Patrick. He reached across Omri, and before Omri could say or so anything, he had slammed the door shut and turned the key. Then, while Omri was still standing there staring, he turned the key again, opened the door, took out Little Bear's figure, and put the double figure of Boone and Ruby Lou on the horse in instead.

"Wait, what are you doing!" Omri exclaimed anxiously.

"Just showing you what's going to happen while you're gone," Patrick remarked calmly.

"What do you mean?"

Patrick turned and squared up to Omri. "Now get this straight," he said between his teeth. "I've decided I'm going to do what you want. I think it's lousy of you to expect it, but I'll do it. But remember, I'm in control. And in the meantime, I'm not just going to sit back here pretending to be ill or whatever. I'm going to be having some fun of my own."

"Well, I'm going to take the key, so you—"

"No, Om. You're not going to take the key so I—anything. I'm going to take the key, and then we're going 'camping.' "

With that, he took the key out of the lock, and slipped it in his pocket.

Omri was so shocked that for a moment he just stood there. He'd seen Patrick mad before, or acting recklessly, but he suddenly saw that as people get older their characteristics—bad as well as good—become more pronounced. Patrick had always been capable of behaving like this, but now he was big (bigger than Omri—he was halfway through his growth shoot) all sides of his character were growing with his body.

For a second Omri wanted to fight him for the key. But he knew he'd lose. And his sense of fairness told him that Patrick had a justifiable grievance. Just the same . . . Omri was not about to walk away and leave all his own little people at Patrick's disposal. Anything could happen.

He pulled himself together.

"Right," he said. "Since you've *stolen* the key, I can't stop you. But you're not going to mess with *my* little people." He picked up the plastic bag, put Little Bear into it, and stared Patrick in the face.

"Please get out of my room," he said.

"So you can hide them. Okay. Go ahead."

Patrick turned on his heel and strode to the door. There he paused, and without looking around, said, "I should hide them really well, if I were you." Then he went out.

The second the door closed, Omri rushed to the fireplace and, reaching up, hid the plastic bag on the ledge inside the chimney. Then he heard his dad calling. He hurried through the door, not noticing he had left sooty fingerprints on the white paint.

They drove slowly, so that Patrick could note the way. Patrick seemed quite cooperative and friendly now.

As they bumped up the cart track toward the crown of trees at the pinnacle of the hill, he leant out of the window. "You can see your place from here. What if I just cut straight down through those fields, instead of going by the road? Be much shorter."

"What will you say—have you thought?" asked Omri's father.

"Oh, yes. I've worked it all out. The thing is, the others are supposed to think you're on Dartmoor, right? So if I just walk back and tell them I threw up or had a row or whatever, they'll have to know where you are."

Omri and his dad looked at each other. "That's right. So?"

"So. I'm not going back today. I'm going to camp here overnight."

"On your own? Are you sure?"

"I'm used to camping in our orchard at home, sometimes with my brother but often by myself. It's nothing.
Then tomorrow I'll kick around—I've got my Walkman
and a magazine and I'll have the food—and then, in the
afternoon, I'll walk back down there and say we all went
for a hike on the moor and we got separated, and I got
completely lost in some mist and couldn't find you or
the camping site. I'll say I spent the day hunting for
you and in the end, I just decided to come back here,
and got a series of lifts as far as your village with the
help of a map. I'll make myself look all worn-out and
grotesque." Omri was staring at him. He seemed to be
his old self, entering into the spirit of this new adventure with relish.

"But if we'd lost you, we'd have to report it and send
out search parties," objected Omri's dad.

"Ah," said Patrick. That stumped him, but only for a
moment. "I know! I'll say that I left a message for you
with the police that I was okay and had gone back to
your place."

"The police wouldn't let you go alone."

"Okay! Right! So the police drove me. If I say that, I
won't even have to make myself look as if I'd walked
half the way."

"My wife," said Omri's father slowly, "is going to smell
a rat. But I think it's the best we can do. Here we are."

The car came to a stop right at the top of Peacock
Hill, resting in a little hollow, invisible from below. They
got out and ran up the slope onto a bank that nearly
surrounded the hollow, all but the track entrance. Trees
that Omri had seen from afar grew out of the bank in a
rough circle, the "peacock's crown" that Omri had often

looked at from his room. Their roots protruded from the earth like a giant's knuckles.

The boys stood staring around. It was a glorious spot. In every direction, the hills, fields, woods, and farms of this most beautiful part of England, marked out irregularly by hedges, stretched away, bathed in morning sunlight. To the south, behind them, could be seen, three times between three pairs of hills, a dazzling line—the sea.

Turning back, Omri could pick out the thatched roof of home nestling below. As he watched, a tiny figure emerged from under the thatch and moved among the flower beds—his mother. Gillon came out after her, turned away, and must have crossed the lane. . . . They looked, as the cattle and sheep in the fields looked, like living toys.

As Omri thought those words, he shivered. Soon that was what they would be—living toys. As small to Little Bear and his people as his mother now looked to him. Unconsciously he reached out his hand as if to pick her up, trying to get the sense of her as small, not the strong person he knew her to be, but helpless in his hand.

Patrick said, "Yes, she looks like I felt when Ruby Lou pickled me up in Texas. You'll be like that soon. Only it won't be so civilized."

"Indians had their own kind of civilization," said Omri.

Patrick grunted. "Come to that, I don't think white people were very civilized. They weren't in Boone and Ruby's time. One of them tried to shoot me the moment he saw me, and most of the others were dead drunk."

Omri turned to him. "Have you changed your mind about wanting to come back with me first?"

"Yes."

"Why? We could go now. Right now."

"I'll pass, thanks."

"Why?" asked Omri again. "You were so keen."

"I've decided I'd rather be the big one," said Patrick. "Besides, Little Bear didn't want me. Nor do you two. You want to have your adventure without me."

This was true and Omri couldn't deny it. But he felt worse than ever, when Patrick was being so nice about it . . . all of a sudden.

Omri's dad, behind them, said urgently, "Come on, we're wasting precious time!" They turned and ran down the slope, letting the side of the car bring them up short.

Omri opened the front passenger door. His father had been arranging things. He'd put two of the sleeping bags on the seat so Omri would be sitting on them. On the floor was a box containing food, a couple of books, and some other things underneath that Omri couldn't see.

"Put your behind on these, and your feet on that," his father was saying. "I've got Little Bear's belt in my shirt pocket. Now. We have to hang onto each other, so the belt will take us both back. Put your anorak on. It's October. It's cold in New York State in October." He swung himself into the driving seat, removed the spare key from the ignition, put it carefully away in the glove compartment, and produced *the* key.

Patrick stood by the car and watched silently.

It seemed Omri's dad, in his eagerness, had forgotten there was ever any question of Patrick and Omri going back together first. He put the key in the ignition. "Patrick, would you like to turn it?"

"Yes," said Patrick steadily. "I'd love that." Omri

glanced at him quickly but his face was blank. "Are you ready?"

Omri's dad turned to look at him. His face was flushed, his breath coming fast. "This is the greatest adventure of them all!" he said. "Are you ready, bub?"

Omri swallowed hard, and nodded.

His father took hold of his hand. Omri couldn't tell who the trembling was coming from—both of them, probably.

"Do it!"

Patrick reached calmly in through the window and turned the key.

15

Howl of a Wolf

Silence and darkness.

Omri breathed deeply to calm the fear. The air caught unpleasantly in his throat and nose for a split second, nearly making him cough, then struggled into his lungs. It was full of strange smells, so strong they were almost tastes. The principal one was smoke.

He found he was lying on his back. He stared upward. He perceived some light now, but despite the open-air cold, it wasn't starlight. A dull reddish glow from somewhere away to his left showed him after some moments that far above his head was an arched roof made of bark.

As his ears became sensitized to the quiet he realized there were sounds. Seemingly from several directions at once came loud snores. Nearer, there were other breathing noises. A slight rustle, as if someone turned over in sleep. A night bird cried. Then, far away but still spine-chillingly, a wolf howled.

Omri cautiously rolled over, then sat up sharply. His eyes had adjusted now. Some way down what looked like an endless tunnel, running off into total darkness, he could see a fire, burning low. By its faint, ruddy glow, he could see, at regular intervals along the tunnel, posts as thick as the thickest oak trunk. Between some pairs of these hung things like curtains, but they were not of cloth. One of them hung near him and he touched it. It was made of some stiff but smooth stuff, with ridges, a bit like paper. He couldn't make out what it was.

He felt a draft of cold air. Instinctively he put his arms around his body. Then he looked down at himself and got a shock.

He was naked.

His first instinct was to hide. He scrambled over the earth floor and ducked under the curtain. Beyond it was deeper darkness, but he could make out a sort of room with a raised section against the wall. On this was a mountain range covered with fur in the shape of a sleeping giant.

Omri stared all around, feeling the beginnings of panic.

"Dad!" he whispered as loudly as he dared.

There was no answer. Omri felt intensely vulnerable with no clothes on. Cold air embraced his skin from head to foot. He felt a sudden longing to go home. He hadn't reckoned on this—being separated from his dad, it being night, so dark and cold, so strange, so lonely.

He made himself start to think.

He was in a longhouse, he knew that much. He remembered reading that the old-style longhouses were very long indeed, with many families living in partitioned compartments on either side of a wide central aisle with a number of fires down the middle. This must be Little Bear's living space. He was expecting them. He wouldn't have just left the man doll lying anywhere. He would keep it near to him. Perhaps it was him, lying asleep under the furs?

Omri stood up beside the raised section, which he realized was a sleeping platform. The top of it was over his head. That made him try to reckon out how big he was, compared to the people here. If a full-sized person was lying asleep under these hides, he himself must be about six or seven inches high. That gave him a great advantage over people who brought to life plastic figures only three inches tall.

He needed Little Bear—if it was him—to wake up, to take care of him. What if it wasn't Little Bear? Well, he must take a chance.

He ran from one end of the platform to the other, a distance, to him, of about twenty yards. There seemed no way he could climb up onto it. Then he almost bumped into something at one end—a basket, upside-down. Standing up close, he could smell it—a flowery, dryish smell, like hay but sweeter. It was enormous, with little woven braids crossing around its sides in a pattern. Omri explored it by touch. The weave was stiff, quite strong enough to make a ladder for him. He clambered up, feeling the woody edges firm under his hands and feet. Soon he stood on the gently sloping bottom of the basket, and now there was another sweet smell— Omri recognized it—it was an herb his mum used for stuffing chicken. Sage.

From here it was an easy step onto the platform where the mountains of fur were, and he knew at once he was at the head-end of their sleeping place because he could feel, against his bare skin, a coming-and-going warmth—human breath. He reached forward and touched flesh.

It twitched. He felt it with his hand. It was a nose. What if it wasn't Little Bear's? He had to take a chance.

He moved his hand, feeling for the eyelid. The eyelashes brushed his fingers. They were opening! Now he saw the faint reflection of light in the white of an eye.

The next moment there was a violent movement—an eruption among the hides—and a hand shot out and seized him.

He got a terrible fright, and for a moment everything seemed to go black. Then, as the warmth of the hand permeated his cold body, he heard a familiar voice.

"Om-ri?"

The voice was now deep and powerful, a man's voice, though it was kept low. Omri realized he had never heard or seen Little Bear full-size before.

"Yes! It's me, Little Bear! I've come!"

The hand released him, and Omri became aware of the big man lying on his side, looking him up and down. Then he heard a deep-throated chuckle.

"You forget to bring clothes?"

"I had some when I started."

"Ah," Little Bear murmured. "Bright Stars must have a plan." He turned over where he lay, shook someone lying asleep beyond him, and spoke some quiet words. There was another eruption among the skins, and Omri, looking far up, saw Bright Stars sitting up behind Little Bear, her hair tumbling around her startled face. He shrank down, covering himself with his hands.

Bright Stars peered at him, put her face against Little Bear's shoulder, and giggled. She spoke to Little Bear, who said, "Wife says, when day comes she will greet you and give clothes. Father also have bare skin?"

"I don't know where he is."

Little Bear chuckled. "I know."

He thrust his hand among the furs that wrapped him and Bright Stars, and Omri heard the sleepy protesting whimper of a small child who must be lying between them. The next moment Little Bear's hand emerged with Omri's dad in it, naked as a jaybird. Omri heard him gasping for breath as if he'd come out of deep water.

"Omri! Are you there?"

"Yes, Dad!" Omri hissed back. "Shhh! Don't shout!" Luckily the shout was a small shout to match his body.

Little Bear gently set Omri's dad down beside him. "I've nearly suffocated! I thought I had no face again! I couldn't imagine where I was or what was happening. It was like being trapped in between two damp hot-air balloons!"

"I think Tall Bear was cuddling you under the skins," said Omri.

"He needs his nappy changed. . . . God, it's cold out here! Where are we? Why are we nake'd?"

His father always said "naked" as if it were the past of a verb "to nake." It was a silly family joke and somehow it made Omri feel better. He almost laughed himself. "I think Bright Stars forgot to put clothes on the man dolls."

"Maybe it was a protest at having to break the taboo and give us faces! Where are all the things we were supposed to bring with us? We've got some spare gear if we could find those. It was you who was touching them."

Omri led the way back to the place on the floor where he had first arrived. Now that his eyes were used to the dark (though they were stinging because of the smoky air) he could see a shape on the ground.

"Look—there they are!"

He and his dad fell on the box and the sleeping bags and dragged them under the curtain. Just as when the little people came to them, the things they had brought were in scale. Omri silently thanked the magic as he groped in the box and found the flashlight, the candles, some tinned food—and a couple of sweaters.

"How are we going to open these tins?" Omri asked as he struggled into his sweater. "Oh, of course—the tin opener on your knife."

"Is the knife there?" asked his dad with sudden anxiety.

"Isn't it in your pocket?"

"My poor idiot, I haven't *got* a pocket, have I?"

"Dad! Does that mean all the stuff you had in your clothes isn't here? The matches?"

"Nope."

A thought struck Omri. "What about the wampum belt?"

"If we had brought it, would it be our size or Little Bear's?"

"His. It came from here."

"How could it bring us and then disappear? It must have got lost on the way."

"Dad!"

"Don't blame me."

"I don't, but I bet Little Bear will!"

The sleeping bags were there, however, and they lost no time in carrying them to the foot of the sleeping platform, and crawling in. Omri was shivering so much his teeth chattered.

"Dad . . . Why is it night here?"

"It's the same time difference as always. It must be nearly morning though—ten A.M. our time in England would be about five A.M. theirs."

"So why am I so tired?"

"Well, it can't be jet lag, can it," said his father dryly. Omri snuggled into the sleeping bag, curling his icy feet round each other. His dad said thoughtfully, "It isn't so scary the second time. But I still find that weird sensation—that feeling of going out of much more than just your body—quite unnerving. And then finding myself clutched to that baby's stomach with his hot little hands . . . No doubt it's just the beginning. I wonder what's in store for us 'come the dawn.' "

"I'm glad you're with me, Dad," mumbled Omri.

"I wish I had my Swiss Army knife."

A short time later, the wolf howled again, but Omri wasn't awake to hear it.

Neither he nor his dad felt themselves being gently lifted and laid in a safer place. In the morning they woke to find themselves in a vast room, curtained-off on three sides and walled with tiles of bark on the fourth. Omri could see what the curtains were, now: they were dried corn husks plaited together.

Tall Bear, a giant one-year-old, was gazing at them from above. Little Bear was behind him, restraining him by holding his hands firmly to his sides.

Omri stared at Little Bear. He was of course huge, but also very handsome. His head was shaven above his ears and his plaited hair fell from the crown; he wore earrings which presumably had always been too small for Omri to see, hanging from holes in his ears large enough for Omri to have put his fist through. His torso was bare and tattooed with faint, curving lines, crossed with several necklaces of leather, beads, and shells. He was smiling.

"You sleep much," he said. "Long journey! Now it is time to greet you."

He lifted the baby and stood aside. To Omri's—and his father's—intense embarrassment, they now saw Bright Stars looming above them. She was holding a wooden basin. She sat down on the edge of the bed and, before either of them could realize what she was doing, she took a piece of soft cloth out of the water in the basin, squeezed it, and began to wash Omri's father with it!

He was so overcome, he couldn't move. He simply stood there with his eyes tightly closed. Omri tried to escape, but Little Bear blocked his flight with a hand as big as a five-barred gate. He turned against it and watched, abashed, as Bright Stars dried his dad and . . . began to dress him!

It was like a ritual. As she did it, she was murmuring soft words in her own language, like a chant. She fastened a belt round his waist, then gave him a long piece of doeskin, butter-yellow and flexible as satin, indicating that he should draw it between his legs and hang the ends over the belt. Then she helped him step into a pair of leggings. By this time he had got over his shame, and was actively helping, fastening the leggings to the belt himself. The moccasins were circles of soft doeskin with braided grass to tie them around the ankles.

When that was done, the moment Omri had been dreading arrived: Bright Stars turned to him. She had his clothes in her hands.

"I—I'll do it myself, Bright Stars!" he croaked. But it was no use. He had to go through the ritual wash first, and be dried, and spoken to, and then he was allowed to dress himself. He was aware of his father standing near him chuckling under his breath.

"It's no use being ashamed," he said quietly. "This is their way with guests, I imagine. We just have to go along with it. It's—er . . . It's really not so bad."

"Dad!"

"No, I mean—we're all far too prudish about our bodies."

Little Bear, who had gone away for a while, returned. "Wife says, not easy to make small clothes. Polite now to say good words to her."

They both thanked Bright Stars and said the clothes were beautiful. Which they were. But their chests were left bare.

"Is there anything for up top?" asked Omri's dad, touching his chest.

"No. Mohawk men wear nothing there."

"Even in winter?"

Little Bear picked up a large piece of fur-covered hide from the bed, and threw it across his shoulders as a cloak. "When winter come, wife make fur clothes," he assured them. They looked at each other.

"We won't be here in the winter," Omri said.

"Meanwhile we've got our sweaters."

But when they put them back on, Little Bear let out a roar of laughter. Bright Stars covered her face to hide her giggles. They stared at each other, and then, without a word, took them off again. Neither of them could have explained it, but even at the cost of being cold, it didn't look right or feel right to wear non-Indian clothes.

"Now we talk," said Little Bear.

He stood up—far, far up, till his head was as high above them as a cliff top—and, leaving Bright Stars smiling and Tall Bear playing on the earth floor, he swooped on them and picked them up.

Omri was made sick and dizzy by the speed with

which he was lifted high above the safe earth, and he heard his father gulp and gasp. Little Bear held them, one in each hand, in front of his handsome face.

"You want food?"

"Not just now," Omri's father managed to croak.

"Good. Talk first."

Little Bear stuck them without ceremony into his belt, wrapped his cloak around him to hide them, and they heard the dry rustle of the corn husks as he brushed past the curtain, moved swiftly beyond the room and, quite shortly, out into the open air.

16

Perfidious Albion

When Little Bear strode with them up a steep hill and into a thick belt of trees, Omri felt almost hit in the face by the impact of the long-ago forest.

It was very different from the ones around the Hidden Valley where he lived. There was a feeling you never got in England, of wildness, of *wilderness*. The trees were familiar—many were the oaks and beeches and willows and ash trees he knew. But there were others, so brilliantly colored that, with the sun shafting through their leaves, Omri could scarcely look at them. It was like being roofed by jewel-colored glass. The air was glassy, too. It was so clear, and after the smoky, smells-laden air in the longhouse, it prickled in his lungs like frost crystals.

There was also a subtle feeling that the forest was somehow *alive,* and that was scary. Of course, being small didn't help.

But being close to Little Bear's strong, warm body did.

Little Bear sat down on a gigantic fallen tree, took them out of his belt, and set them one on each thigh. Omri found it was like straddling a whale. He glanced at the ground. It was a long way away. His fingers searched for something to cling to, finding only the smoothness of stretched buckskin. But Little Bear kept a guardian finger and thumb looped loosely around him.

The Indian began to speak. In fact, he seemed to be making a speech. His voice boomed out far above them. When they gazed upward, they could see the jerks of his Adam's apple like the prow of a ship moving sharply with the waves. But his voice flowed over their heads and was drowned by the cries of birds, the whirring of a million insects, and the loud rustle of twigs, leaves, and branches in the forest canopy, which was sky-high above them.

Omri's dad leant toward Omri across the gap.

"Can you hear what he's saying?"

"Not properly."

"Tell him."

"You."

Omri's dad put his head back and shouted. Little Bear took no notice. Omri had an idea, and thumped with both fists against the huge thumb that encircled his waist.

Little Bear, startled, looked down, then bent toward them. The sudden appearance of his enormous face close above them made them cower.

"What?" he said. It came out as a roar that lifted the hair on their heads.

"We can't hear you, Little Bear! Come down to us!"

The next moment they were lifted to dizzy heights; then the ground—covered with a glorious pattern of bright five-pointed leaves as big as hearth rugs—rushed toward them as Little Bear stretched himself at full length on the forest floor. He put them down, and they sat on the colored leaves. It was like sitting on an endless leathery carpet of reds, oranges, yellows, browns, and greens. The crisp air chilled their bare chests, and they hugged themselves.

"I wait," said Little Bear clearly. "I wait before make move. I wait for *you*. But now, not wait more. I must decide for my people. We cannot stay here. There is much danger."

"What is the danger?" asked Omri's dad.

"English soldiers go home and leave us. People of the Longhouse are alone."

There was a pause. He scowled, as if suddenly remembering that *they* were English. But if so, it didn't hold him back.

"They promise very much, for our help. Weapons. Blankets. Trade goods. Pay from English king. They use fine words: 'No Indian child cold again. No Indian woman hungry.' *Ha!* So we fight. First the French. Then other Indians. We beat them. English thanked us! But as we fight, all is changing. White men come, more than hunters and traders, men with hunger for our land— many, many—come here from across the big water. Bad men. They call us savages, then teach us what that word means. Cheat, lie, do very evil things.

"Then English king's men come again to us. Again they need us, to fight these bad people. They call them 'rebels'—men who hate English king and want to stay here and drive Indians out with tricks and lies, with white man's sickness, with whiskey, with guns, with fire."

"The settlers," said Omri's father under his breath

to Omri. "The European settlers who were starting to be American."

Little Bear didn't hear him.

"This time we tread the warpath with hot blood, more than before. We hate these people. They are like fire in forest, river that forgets its path, that grows and grows and swallows everything. They move always toward the sunset—"

"Westward—"

"They cut down our trees, drive away our hunt animals, burn our corn. Kill and do worse than kill."

He turned his face away and his voice dropped.

"Om-ri. You asked one time about wife. Wife who is gone from me."

"Yes. You told me she'd died."

"Yes. But not how. Now you will listen. White savages come and burn our crops. They take my wife. *Take* her. You understand me? When found, she was not dead. She ask me to end her shame. I could not. But she—" He stopped and did not go on for a long time. They saw his throat move as the muscles tightened. "She choose her own ending. This eat me like the lump sickness. White men do this who call Indians dogs. This the Indian does not do to woman—never.

"So we fight these rebels. Burn and kill like them. And they fall to our warriors like deer. We drive them back and back. Their blood wash our land clean and it become again our land. This is our fight, but England's also. We look that the king's men keep their word! And then—*whaaah!*—the English say 'finish.' They give up and go."

"They knew they'd lost their colony," muttered Omri's dad. He was looking very uncomfortable. As if he was

ashamed. *But why?* thought Omri. *What the English did hundreds of years ago wasn't our fault.*

"Couldn't you go on fighting the settlers without them?" he asked.

"The English have clever talk to make us take warpath, now they make new talk. They say, 'We go home. No more war.' They say, 'Plant again the great Tree of Peace, bury weapons as Iroquois did long ago, when the Peacemaker ordered that we do not fight Mohawk against Onondaga, Oneida against Cayuga and Seneca.' English say we must make new Confederacy, this time with rebels. This is their counsel! But these are not Indian brothers to bring to the white roots of our Peace Tree! They are our enemies, forever. Anger burns our hearts. We want to fight. But we cannot follow warpath now without English weapons or other things we need. We cannot fight bows and arrows against guns. And our guns are empty.

"And rebels' fire burns against us again. More hot than before, because now they want vengeance. We have no supplies. Many fields black with fire. Fruit trees cut. Our stomachs grow small. We must stand on our land against their guns, as in the beginning of the white man's coming. Or we must find new hunting grounds where white men cannot follow."

"And you need to decide where to go," said Omri's father.

"Yes. That. And to turn angry young warriors from warpath when they want to fight without hope to win. Who will father new children if all our young men are dead?"

There was a pause in the conversation. Omri looked into Little Bear's smooth golden face in the flickering, shifting light. It was not just the cold that made him shiver, because for seconds at a time it seemed as if Little Bear vanished. The light would flash on him, showing his dark, anxious, expectant eyes. Then, again, he would disappear into a shadow.

A thought he couldn't explain or suppress seemed to write itself across Omri's mind: *Desperate. He feels desperate. We owe him. We must help.* But wasn't this as ludicrous as Little Bear saying to him, the first time he ever saw him, "You touch—I kill"? What could they possibly do to help?

At last Omri's father said, "Which of the Six Nations of the Iroquois do you belong to, Little Bear?"

"Three eagle feathers stand in my *gustoweh.* I am Mohawk, elder brother among our nations."

"I need to look up some things in my books."

"You bring paper that talks about what will come?"

"Yes. I want to see what the Mohawks actually did. Of course that doesn't mean your longhouse couldn't do something different."

Back in the longhouse, in the compartment belonging to Little Bear's family, Omri and his father were left alone with their things. They were shielded by a stack of baskets, in a corner by the bark wall.

Omri's father immediately sat down cross-legged on the earth floor. Omri thought he looked strange in his Indian clothes, like an actor who's forgotten to fix his hair and take off his watch. Indians' skin, he'd noticed, was not red at all, but it wasn't white either, and his father really looked like a "paleface."

He took *Stolen Continents* out of the box they'd brought. It had bits of paper sticking out, marking places, and he opened it to one of these, putting his face right down to the page. Omri realized he had lost his glasses when he lost his own clothes.

"What are you reading, Dad?"

"I want to find out what happened with the Mohawks. I seem to remember some of them had settled in Canada long before the Revolutionary War. And the British promised more land around Lake Ontario, to keep forever, as a reward for their help. I just have to see what happened to them, and whether our lot could join them. It'd get Little Bear out of the way of the horrors that are coming to the Indians who stay here, anyway." He looked at Omri and said soberly, "This is such a terrible moment for them. You can't imagine how powerful the Iroquois were once! How well organized and what ferocious fighters. They claimed to have conquered half this country, before it was a country. And now they're facing annihilation. Let me read, Omri."

He became immersed in his book.

Omri knew he should stay close to him, but he was restless. And hungry! He sniffed. Through the strong smells of bark, smoke, sage, and smoked skins came a rich, meaty smell. The clean, cold air of the woods had sharpened his appetite. This morning they'd foraged in the box, and found nothing. The tins of meat and beans and soup mocked their lack of a tin opener, and Omri thought enviously of Patrick, tucking into the stuff in the cooler.

He drifted toward the smell of stew. Just to get a better whiff of it. He knew he mustn't break cover, but if he just put his head under the cornhusk curtain . . .

The next second something huge pounced on him, and gigantic teeth closed around his body.

17

The Old Woman

A wave of absolute terror went over Omri.

He was snatched from the ground and borne along. He guessed at once that it was a dog that had pounced on him—he had seen or at least heard dogs around the longhouse—and he managed to stay perfectly still. He felt instinctively that if he struggled, its great teeth would close and he would be bitten in half, and the thought was enough to paralyze him.

As it was, he was held tightly—he could feel the teeth digging into him without piercing the skin—and carried at speed along the aisle, to him as wide as a six-lane highway, between the family compartments toward one of the central fires.

Halfway there, his fear-frozen brain came to his aid.

He was small, rat-size to the dog, but he was not a rat—he was a human being and he must smell like one. Perhaps that was why the dog had not simply eaten him on the spot. The scent of human would confuse it.

In a flash he remembered the old man who'd lived next door to them in the last London house. He'd had a dog. It was very obedient and well trained. He'd used to throw things for it to chase, in his garden next to theirs. When it brought the ball or stick or whatever it was, it would stand in front of the man, who would say in stern tones: "Drop it! Drop it, I say!"

Omri had once peered over the fence and asked him if the dog understood his words. "More the tone of voice, actually," the man had replied. "So if you said it in French, he'd still do it?" "Can't speak a word of French," the man had said shortly, "so we'll never find out."

And Omri couldn't speak a word of Iroquoian.

The dog holding Omri slowed down as it came near the fire. Omri felt the heat scorching his skin and instinctively twisted his head to look. To him it looked like a blazing forest. The smell of stew was very strong now—there was a cauldronlike pot hanging from a hook over the smoldering side logs.

What if he said, "Drop it!" to the dog, and it dropped him—into the red-hot embers?

The dog stood still. It turned its head, with Omri still firmly held between its teeth. It seemed to be looking for something—waiting for an order. Omri made up his mind. When the dog's head was turned away from the fire, Omri shouted: "Drop it! Drop it now!"

For a split second the teeth tightened and Omri thought his last moment had come. But then, quite gently, the dog bent its head and laid Omri on the ground.

He lay there, his heart nearly bursting out of his ribs. There was slobber all over his torso, and bruises wherever the teeth had been. He felt himself gingerly, while the dog sniffed at him, but somehow respectfully now.

It's a dog, thought Omri. *That's all it is. Just a stupid old dog.*

He got up slowly, his eyes on the dog. He noticed it was white all over, and of a breed he had never seen before. It backed away, whining softly.

"Get lost!" Omri shouted commandingly. "Push off! Scram!"

The dog's hair suddenly bristled, and Omri thought he had made the worst mistake of his life. But then it turned, tail between legs, and slithered under the nearest corn-husk curtain, yelping with fear.

Omri stood near the fire, dry-mouthed, shaking, and tried to recover himself. He knew he should get back straight away to Little Bear's cubicle, but he didn't know which one it was and for him it was quite a long walk, a walk fraught with danger all the way. Besides, the smell of stew, and the warmth of the fire, held him as long as he felt weak from his scare.

Just then he became aware of a movement. He turned his head sharply, and saw that someone was watching him.

She was sitting right at the other side of the fire. An old, old woman. He hadn't seen her before because part of the fire with its drifting smoke was between them, and she was quite still—a dark, hunched figure with a wooden ladle in one hand and a bowl in the other, just watching him through the smoke.

She wasn't so much staring as peering at him through the smoke, with narrowed eyes. A long time seemed to pass. Then she rose slowly and hobbled around the fire to where he was standing.

She crouched down again. Her knees beneath their

ancient buckskin skirt rose on either side of him like hills. He gazed up into a face that reminded him of the cliffs on the shore of the English Channel near his home—reddish sandstone eroded by rain into long downward creases. This face was like a wind carving in that cliff, wrinkled beyond anything he had ever seen. She looked about a hundred and twenty years old. Her eyes were swollen and inflamed; Omri saw that she couldn't make him out properly because she kept turning her head this way and that. But she was smiling an ancient smile.

She put the bowl down and a palsied hand groped for him. Before he could think what to do, she had picked him up.

She lifted him level with her face and examined him. She turned him this way and that and felt him with her bony fingers. She was smiling and shaking her head wonderingly. She spoke to him. Of course he didn't answer. Her face registered impatience.

Suddenly her shaking hand lost its hold and he found himself dangling by one leg! He let out a yell. She swung him right way up again, and again she asked him a question. He shrugged, the big, neck-shrinking shrug his dad did sometimes, using his hands. The old woman grinned crazily. She had one huge tooth, the size of a tombstone.

Her face was so full of childlike pleasure, he felt emboldened somehow. He pointed to his mouth. She nodded, still grinning, and put him in her lap, which was like a vast hammock. She reached up and scooped something out of the pot with the ladle, and brought it down to him.

The ladle was like a small murky lake full of islands. The liquid was gravy, the islands were lumps of meat and vegetables. It was steaming hot. The old woman let out a cackle, and with heat-proof finger and thumb she broke off a pinch of meat and blew on it. Then she dumped it into Omri's arms. He yelled again! It was like having half a barbecued pig to hold.

It was burning his arms, and smearing them all over with grease and gravy, but this was bearable next to his hunger. The smell pulled his teeth to the meat like a magnet and he took a bite. It was marvelous! He gnawed on the long fibers of the meat and the juices spilled into his eager mouth. He tore at it until he could eat no more, while the old woman made little gurgling noises of amusement.

She took the last of it away from him and ate it herself. She wiped her fingers on the ground. Then the "hills" and the earth floor sank away as she levered herself upright, still holding Omri tightly. She turned— she was going to take him off to her own compartment. Omri knew it and felt almost as fearful as when he had been in the power of the dog.

But suddenly, right in front of him, he saw a familiar necklace.

He strained to look upward. Yes! It was Little Bear, standing close in front of the old woman.

He spoke to her, respectfully but strongly. He put out his hand—it was within reach of Omri. There was a pause. He felt the old woman's clawlike fingers clenching him possessively. He gasped—he felt the breath being squeezed out of him. Little Bear laid his hand on the old woman's and he spoke again, very gently. He was asking her to give Omri up. . . . The squeezing clutch relaxed, and, with a reluctance Omri could sense, she handed him over.

The relief was overwhelming! He instantly felt safe

again. He almost kissed Little Bear's hand as once again it encircled his waist. Little Bear went striding down the aisle, and in a few moments, Omri felt the rustling curtain brush against his face and they were back in the compartment.

Little Bear then held Omri up in front of him and proceeded to give him the bollocking of all time.

"You! You stay with father! Stay where you are safe! You are boy and Little Bear is man, but when in your world, he stays, does not run alone looking for danger! If you die Little Bear will cry. Bright Stars cry. Father cry. And how your father will help our tribe if he cries over your body? Stupid. Stupid!"

"I was hungry," said Omri sulkily.

Little Bear looked taken aback. "No one give food?"

"No."

Little Bear grunted thoughtfully and set him down next to his father, who looked white-faced and torn between anger and relief. "Where the hell did you go?" he muttered. "Omri! What happened to you, you're covered with bruises!"

"A dog picked me up."

Omri's father turned a shade paler, if possible, and simply stared at him in horror. He looked almost ill. He put his arms around Omri and held him for a moment. "Don't. Don't," he muttered into his ear. Omri understood what he couldn't say. "I won't, Dad. I'm sorry."

They sat down among the hide hills together in silence.

After a few minutes, Bright Stars came through the curtain with a bowl in her hand and laid it before them. It was full of the same stew. Omri's father perked up a bit. "Hey, smell that," he said rather weakly. Omri was feeling terrible about having frightened him and tried

to get over it with a joke. "I'm an Indian stew!" he sang.
"Try it, Dad. It's good."

But his dad was more cautious. "What is this meat?"
he asked Bright Stars.

She smiled and touched some decoration on her dress.

"Does she mean it's deer?"

"No," said his dad. "I'm afraid not. Those are quills.
This must be porcupine meat."

Omri swallowed. "Well, it's really good, anyway."

"How do you know?"

"A crazy old woman gave me some."

Whoosh!

He left his stomach, full of the oily meat, far behind
him as Little Bear snatched him up again. It was like
going up in an elevator at the rate of twenty floors a
second.

"Bad words!" roared Little Bear, shaking him fiercely.
"You do not call woman crazy! She is Eldest Clan
Mother! Full of wisdom, full of years! You show her respect or I bring dog, and drop no tears when he eats
you!"

Omri tried to hold the contents of his stomach down
but it was no use. The shaking was the last straw, and
he threw up violently. This brought Little Bear out of his
anger, if only because he had to thrust Omri hastily away.

There was a pause and then he burst out laughing.
"Now you need more food, fill empty stomach! Soon no
more food for tribe!" he said.

Omri uttered a groan and wiped his mouth, thinking
irresistibly of his tiny pellet of sick, probably still on its
long journey to the ground. Little Bear set him down
more gently.

"You and father eat," he said. "Then father tell what
his talking paper says will come."

"Are you all right, bub?" asked his father anxiously as Omri was restored to him.

"More or less," said Omri. "I didn't know she was a clan mother. It's clan mothers who choose the chiefs—probably she chose Little Bear. No wonder he was so polite to her."

He glanced at the huge lake of stew at whose shores his father had begun to feast, and then hurriedly away again. Noticing his green face, Omri's dad stopped eating. Omri half expected to see him wipe his fingers on the ground, Indian-fashion, but he rubbed the grease carefully into his hands instead. It didn't seem right to wipe them on any of the skins or on his new clothes.

"What are you going to tell Little Bear?" Omri said after a pause.

His father sighed heavily. "God knows. What a terrible dilemma. I wish I'd stayed well out of it now."

"Why? What did the book say?"

"From what I can make out, there were three ways the Iroquois tribes went at this time. Some of them stayed put and tried to recover their lands or at least to hold out against the settlers, who were steadily moving west and driving them back. I hope Little Bear's people won't do that, because those Indians lost everything. A lot of them were killed, and their way of life was badly damaged. A lot of the tribes who stayed on the fringes of settler territory just succumbed to despair and alcohol and— No. I can't bear to think of that.

"The second thing was, they moved west, trying to get out of the way of the expansion, and joined with other tribes. But that wasn't much good either, because the whites just kept coming up behind them, pushing them farther and farther from their own territories, forcing them to make alliances with tribes whose customs they didn't understand. They tried to fight back, but in the end they were all overtaken by the Europeans anyway. Most of their homelands except for a few tiny patches were taken from them by conquest or by broken treaties. It was just a long-drawn-out agony. Defeat and treachery and poverty—and the worst was that they just didn't know who they were any more. They went through hell. An awful lot of them died of diseases brought by the Europeans. There were some terrible cases of them being infected on purpose, to kill them off. . . ."

Omri shuddered. "And the third way?"

His father brooded for such a long time that Omri began to fear that there was no third way, or that it was just as bad as the other two.

"Dad?"

"Well. The Canada option."

"Moving north?"

"Yes. Especially the Mohawks. There were Mohawks in Canada already, and some of the ones from this area, which became New York State, went up there and joined them."

"What happened to them?"

"They're still around."

Omri sat up straight, queasiness forgotten. "Now? I mean, in our time?"

"Yes. Tens of thousands of Mohawks, and other Iroquois tribes, are living in a few small reservations around the United States-Canada border. They still have their pride and their identity. They even remember their language."

"Dad!" Omri cried excitedly. "Then that's it! That's what you have to advise Little Bear to do!"

He looked into his father's face for some reflection of his own feeling of intense relief. But there was none.

"I don't think," he said very soberly, "that it's up to me to advise them at all. And if I did, I'm not sure I'd want to let them in for—the Canada option."

18

Dreams

"But what did the clan mother think when she saw me?"

Omri and his father were sitting once again on Little Bear's thighs, this time in the "room." Bright Stars was weaving a basket out of thin, pliant strips of white wood; Tall Bear was having his afternoon nap among the furs.

"Clan Mother think you are little man."

"What do you mean?"

"One of small people, living in earth, under bushes, in holes. They have life like us."

Omri and his father exchanged puzzled looks. You could believe strange things more easily here; but what were these "little men"? The Indians' leprechauns? "Do you believe in them?"

"Why this question? They are."

"Have you seen them?"

"Before two moons I see one teasing dog with stick."

"How do they look?"

"Like us. But small."

"How do they dress?"

"As me. As you."

"Lucky I wasn't wearing my sweater!" said Omri. He could see his dad was thinking what he was. Could Little Bear really think he'd seen one?

"Clan Mother spoke of you," Little Bear said presently.

"She said something about me?"

"Yes. She said she saw you in night."

"No one saw us," said Omri's dad, "except you."

"She saw you in dream."

"Oh, a *dream* . . ." said Omri. He thought dreams were a drag.

But his dad leant forward eagerly. "What was her dream, Little Bear?"

"Clan Mother asked me to guess her dream. I try to guess, so then she tell me. Little man came out of ground. Arm straight." He pointed. "Shout without sound. Moving other arm. Like this." Little Bear beckoned strongly. "In dream, Clan Mother called to others. People came out of longhouse. Little man turned and ran away. Still moved arm and showed way."

"As if calling the people to come after him?"

Little Bear nodded slowly, frowning.

"Which way did he run, the little man?"

"To forest."

"Which direction is that? Toward the sunset?"

"No. Toward home of most cold wind."

"North," said Omri's dad quietly to Omri.

* * *

Late in the afternoon, Little Bear took them for a walk.

He didn't cover them with his cloak this time, and the Indians they passed who saw them seemed curious but not surprised. Perhaps the clan mother had passed the word that "little men" were visiting their chief.

They could now see that there was a palisade of sharpened stakes, perhaps twenty feet high, set in the ground tightly together all around the longhouse. There was no gate. The palisade's two ends folded one behind the other, so people could get in or out in single file. Omri couldn't see a back entrance, but he hoped there was one.

Beyond was a large cleared area, with the forest only coming close in one place, on a hill too steep for fields. They could see the stumps of many trees, and among them was a blackened field where, Little Bear explained, the settlers had sneaked up at night a month before and burned their crops. A few sweetcorn plants had survived—now rustling-dry and stripped of cobs. Up the still-upright stalks of the corn plants Omri could see that beans had been growing. And around their bases, there had been—and still were, though the big leaves had been frost-shriveled—more vegetables: squash, like enormous green sausages, and big sun-colored pumpkins that lay among their dry tendrils, big enough to make Cinderella's coach. There were women out picking the smaller ones and putting them into big baskets.

"How come they didn't burn everything?"

"We see fire in night. Run out, making big noise. Shoot with bow and gun, killing three, driving others off. I jumped on horse and followed." Little Bear pointed to his pony, brought back from Omri's time, grazing at a distance. "I killed two more with tomahawk." He put Omri and his dad on the ground, sat cross-legged before them, and with an air of grim satisfaction, pulled two hanks of hair out of his belt.

Omri turned his head away instinctively, but then he made himself look. The hair looked fresh; he could see the dried blood on the scraps of skin at the bottom. He set his teeth against a grimace, and stared steadily at the scalps for a long time, crushing his squeamishness. It helped that he didn't care that those men had been scalped. He felt totally on the Indians' side.

"Now all our bullets are gone," said Little Bear quietly. "Soon rebels will come again. We fight guns with bows, arrows, trade axes. And we are not enough. Many young warriors of tribe are gone from us. To scout, to keep watch for raids. And to raid in vengeance."

"Raids against the settlers?"

Little Bear looked away.

"Not only."

"Who else?"

"Oneida. Cayuga."

"Little Bear, not your own Confederacy tribes!"

"My word was no!" he shouted suddenly. "There was a great quarrel with young warriors! But Little Bear is only pine-tree chief, and our Mohawk are very angry. Oneida, Cayuga help French in war, and now they join with the rebel English. These promise them protection, tell them land is there for them. For us, land is mother, not for belonging. So some Iroquois tribes fight against us on side of rebels. Now Mohawk warriors punish them—burn their villages."

There was a long, long silence. Omri was shocked and scared. He glanced at his dad. He was looking very serious, and heaved a deep sigh.

"Of course that won't help," he said.

"I know this. But young men cannot stay in longhouse and work land like women. Their blood is hot."

"And you?"

"My blood is hot. But head is cold. Hot head is no good. Chiefs must think for all people in longhouse." There was another silence, and at last Little Bear sighed heavily in his turn. "We must leave longhouse. I know this for many moons."

"So why didn't you leave before now?"

"After we leave," Little Bear answered slowly, "longhouse fall down. Fall down forever."

"You mean, yours will."

"No, not only. Iroquois will be no more *Haudenosauree,* People of the Longhouse."

"Little Bear," said Omri's dad carefully, "I'm curious. My books say most Iroquois live in cabins now."

"True. Our village is not like others."

"Why?"

"I have dream also," said Little Bear in a solemn undertone. "After my journey to you a dream came of the Peacemaker who planted Tree of Peace, before many, many harvests. He sits before me and makes ring with his arms. Inside this ring are all my people. His hair blows over them. Then his arms become walls made of skin of tree, and his hair is roof. He changes. *He becomes the longhouse.* I hear his voice say, 'When Mohawk no longer live together as one people, they are no longer People of the Longhouse. Onondaga, Keepers of the Fire, already break fire in two. People scatter one from one, like dry leaf in wind. They no longer talk together in council. No more one people. Hear my words. Longhouse must stay forever.'

"When we travel here from village Algonquin burn,

my people say, they want to live in cabin, one man, one woman, alone with children. My word was no. Many times I speak it, and tell them, guess my dream. They will not guess. So I cannot tell them. They show me their backs and begin to make cabins. So I build long-house alone, as I build once with you. Clan mothers keep closed mouths. No one help me. Many days Little Bear work alone, and village watch. First they laugh. Then they stop and watch without noise. And then Old Clan Mother speaks. 'Little Bear is right. Help him.' "

"And did they help then?" Omri asked.

"Yes. Then many work with me, make longhouse big enough for all. Wood of cabins we burn in longhouse fires. Put up wall of trees, as in time before. For this, they make me pine-tree chief."

"What's a pine-tree chief?" Omri asked.

"True chief is one clan mothers choose. People and other chiefs choose pine-tree chief. Little Bear is not a true chief."

"Who is your true chief?"

He shook his head. "We have no elder chief here now. No one worthy now—so many old ones die of sickness. They take wisdom with them. Pine-tree chief is proud honor. But I have not the old wisdom. Father last con-doled chief."

"Did your father die of the white man's sickness?"

"No. White savage shoot him. *One shot* take from this world all his wisdom, all he know and learn and dream and remember. Perhaps we never again have elder chief. None live long enough."

He sounded achingly sad, as if he saw some deathly end to it all, a chasm down which they were all destined to fall.

Omri's dad went to him and, reaching up, touched his knee.

"Little Bear, don't lose hope. There is a future for your people. My books say so."

Little Bear looked at him for a while. Then he said, "Future. This means, time to come?"

"Yes."

"Because you know this, I ask that you come here."

"Yes, I know."

"For the white man," Little Bear said slowly, "time that is gone, time that is now, time to come, all make one line." He drew a long straight line with his finger in the earth. "For Indian, all time is the same time. Those from time that is gone, are still here, in us. The—future—is with us too, it happens as we happen. Now. When I travel to your time, it is still my time."

Omri's father frowned. "You're saying that time is a kind of spiral." He drew a corkscrew shape in the air. "All happening at once. That's why you weren't surprised when Omri—when the magic—brought you to us."

"Little Bear surprised by many things you have. Not the travel."

"Your ideas are very interesting, Little Bear," Omri's father said humbly.

The Indian straightened suddenly. "But our talk walks away! Tell me my need. Which way must we take to our future?"

Omri's dad looked to see where the sun was going down, and pointed ninety degrees to the right of it.

"The way of the cold wind," he said. "North. Like in Old Clan Mother's dream. Could you collect your people and persuade them to travel north?"

"What is there?"

"More of your people. Mohawk lands. Most land that the white men will give to the Indian will be poor land, but there the land is good. But it's a long way, and there are dangers, till you come to the great river."

"What river?"

"We call it the Saint Lawrence."

"We know of this place. How long is journey?"

"Many days, I should think, with women and children and old people."

Little Bear sniffed the air.

"Soon snow will come."

"Yes. Winter's coming. It'll be hard going. The sooner you leave, the better."

Little Bear tensed. "You read a good future for Mohawk by this great river?"

Omri's dad drew a deep breath.

"Not all the time. White people will cheat you and steal your land. Your people will change. But there will still be a longhouse and Tall Bear's children's children's children will know they're Mohawks and will speak your language and hold to your beliefs—at least, some of them will."

"That is as our field burnt by white men. When fire dies, two hands of corn plants stand against fire and give us their seeds." He held up ten fingers.

"Yes. But so long as a few survive . . . If they're strong enough, they can rebuild the tribe and the longhouse. Little Bear, surely it's better than nothing."

Little Bear thought for only a short time. Then he rose smoothly to his feet and gazed away to the north, where the forested hills, blazing with leaf color in the late sunshine, met the horizon. He stooped, picked them up, and, holding Omri's father level with his face, said, "If they will listen, we will go."

"And your warriors who are away?"

"We leave word. We send messenger. They will follow if they wish. But I think they will stay and fight, and many will die." His voice dropped low. "Little Bear has one wish, that we are of one mind—all the Iroquois. But your word is true. We must put water on our fires and go—north, into the mouth of cold wind."

"You'll build the longhouse again, Little Bear," said Omri's father softly. But Little Bear was staring at the bright forest on the hill and didn't hear him. Omri, held against the Indian's chest by his big hand, could hear his heart beating hard and fast, like a drum, and felt him shiver, as if the deep cold of winter and of strange country had him already in its clutches. As if the protection and comforting familiarity of the longhouse he'd built had already been left far behind.

Omri heard his father whisper, "Oh God. I hope I've done right."

His father was not a believer. But Omri thought that that was the nearest to a prayer he had ever heard him utter.

19

Drums and Fire

On the way back, through the entrance to the stockade and into the longhouse, Little Bear told them they were to witness a ceremony, a ceremony of departure, of farewell to their longhouse, of a great journey to come. That, they thought, would be interest, excitement, experience enough.

They couldn't know the nightmare that lay ahead.

Bright Stars was playing with the baby when they returned to their lodge room, and looked up expectantly. Little Bear spoke to her. Her face showed surprise; but also a sort of relief, as if what she had been expecting had finally happened. She put Tall Bear aside, jumped up immediately, and began folding the furs, but Little Bear stopped her and made some suggestions. She listened carefully, then nodded and pushed through the curtain.

She had finished the basket she'd been making and

had hung it up on one of the poles with all the things Omri and his father had brought with them inside it. Now Little Bear put Omri and his father into it too. It was like being in the basket of a hot-air balloon, high above the ground.

"Safe," Little Bear said tersely, and went out after his wife.

Omri didn't feel particularly safe.

"What's going to happen, Dad?"

"What's going to happen?" repeated his father slowly. "Well. Little Bear will tell his people that they should leave. Then we'll spend the night, and tomorrow's the day Patrick's due to bring us back. End of adventure." But he didn't sound as if he regarded it just as an adventure anymore.

Omri looked over the edge of the basket at the ground far below. He saw something pushing its way under the corn-husk curtain. It was a dog. Tall Bear gave a gurgle of laughter as it wriggled its way toward him, belly to the ground, backside waggling.

"Why are all the dogs here white?" asked Omri, watching from his safe height as the dog and the baby started to play together.

"It's a special breed. The pure white ones are bred for sacrificing."

Omri swung his head round. "*Sacrificing!* You mean, they kill them?"

"Yes."

"Dad!"

"What?"

"That's horrible!"

"Don't be silly, Omri," said his father shortly. "Think of all the animals we kill to eat. This is to please the Great Spirit, which is just as important to the Indians as food. And I'll tell you something else. Every dog they sacrifice has to be somebody's beloved pet, otherwise it doesn't count as a sacrifice at all."

Omri didn't speak for a while. Over the rim of the basket he was watching the little scene below. The dog was rolling on its back, grinning as happy dogs do, its tongue lolling. The baby was pulling its ear rather roughly, but it didn't seem to mind.

Omri thought of the dog who had picked him up. Just a stupid old dog, he'd thought. . . . But some family's pet. He knew animal sacrifice was part of several religions in his own time. Why should it make a difference that the Mohawk did it with *dogs?* It didn't. Omri thought it was horrible whoever did it. Killing to eat was one thing. But for a god? How could you worship a god who wanted something so cruel? He was glad his family wasn't religious! And yet he could see how vitally important it was to the Indians, how much strength it gave them to believe in a creator who cared for them. He felt, not for the first time, that it would be a relief to be able to pray sometimes, especially in times of danger.

He was suddenly shivering. So he put on his sweater and climbed into his sleeping bag. All around him was a lovely scent, sweeter than new hay, drowning out even the smoky smell of their clothes. "What's that smell, Dad?"

"Sweetgrass," said his father. "These dark bits woven into the basket, see? It goes on smelling sweet for ages."

Omri breathed in the scent, and dozed. Then he slept. And he, too, had a dream.

He was in a wood, standing on something high, stretched across a dirt road. He was no longer small. Around him were other men (he knew *he* was a man, not a boy) with rifles, in camouflage uniforms, but despite that, he knew they were Indians. He looked to sce if he was wearing a uniform, but he wasn't; yet hc felt he was one of them, on their side.

Suddenly there were gunshots. He wanted to duck down, behind the barricade, but he couldn't move. He wanted a gun to defend himself, but when he looked down at his hand, it was empty except for a tiny stick. He was sweating with fear, and then the voice of Little Bear spoke to him quietly. It said, "We are of one mind. Your weapon is in your hand." Omri looked again, desperately, and saw the twig was a pencil.

He woke up suddenly. The dream was so real to him still that he was clenching his right hand on the pencil, and when he pulled his hand out of the sleeping bag, he was baffled to see that his fist was empty. Then he felt the basket move slightly.

He looked up at the rim. A giant but distinctly femalc hand was coming in over the fancy edge of the basket. On two of her fingers, like big thimbles, were little caps with feathers all over them. What tiny feathers they must be to her!

"What are these?" Omri's father asked.

"*Gustoweh,*" came Bright Stars's gentle voice from below.

"Ah! For the ceremony. Thanks, Bright Stars. They're beautiful."

Omri sat up, and his father said, "Take off your sweater." He did, and his dad fitted the cap on his head. Then he put on his own. Omri stared at him. Soft curving feathers sprouted from the top of the cap and fell around his father's forehead, neck, and ears, like Not-a-way in the painting. From the crown, three tall straight feathers stuck up. It should have looked funny, but it didn't. His dad didn't look like an Indian, but he didn't look like an actor anymore, either. He looked very solemn. Almost reverent.

"The *gustoweh* are their headdresses. Look. She's even given us three white standing-up feathers. That's because we're Mohawks. The other Iroquois tribes don't have three, because the Mohawks are the elder brothers."

"What do you mean, Dad—we're Mohawks?"

His father frowned. "Did I say—? Sorry, that was ridiculous. I meant—" But he didn't go on.

For the first time, Omri thought it would be a good thing if Patrick didn't wait the two days they'd arranged, but brought them back sooner. He'd heard the expression *going native,* and he thought his dad might be doing it.

When it was dark and the only light came from the fire, they sensed a lot of movement. All around them was the rustling of corn-husk curtains and the murmur of voices, the soft shuffling of moccasins on earth, and the crackling of the fire. They waited. Before long, they felt their basket being lifted off the pole and lowered. Little Bear carried it, and them, out into the main aisle of the longhouse and walked slowly and solemnly into the center where the main fire had been built up. He wore a cloak of hides that shielded the basket from view, but they could peep out and see what was going on as it was carried along.

A large gathering, perhaps forty people including a lot of children, were seating themselves on blankets on the ground, the women on one side of the fire, the men, all wearing their *gustoweh*, on the other. Some of the men carried small drums and rattles. The women wore their best dresses, decorated with beadwork and quill-work, and a lot of shiny silver ornaments.

When everyone was sitting, Little Bear stood up in the center. He closed his cloak around the basket, so that Omri and his father were in smoky-smelling dark-ness, and began to speak. He spoke for a long time. What he said sounded like poetry or a prayer, and after a while Omri noticed that every verse, or paragraph, ended with the same words. Perhaps it was like "amen," because the people joined in.

When he had finished, he sat down and parted his cloak a little so that they could see what was happening. Across the fire, a figure rose up and began to speak. Omri saw who it was—the clan mother.

He had thought her a crazy old woman. But she didn't seem crazy now. She talked like someone who is used to making speeches, and to having them listened to with complete attention. Her voice droned on and on, not hes-itating, not stumbling. Every eye was fixed on her. Even the youngest children were still and silent, with the firelight gleaming in their wide-open eyes. After she'd finished, she looked round at them all. Her sunken, in-flamed eyes were glistening. Was she crying? Her face showed not a trace of emotion. She gave one nod, and sat down again, with some help from the women on either side of her.

Several others, men and women, then spoke. Omri noticed now how few young men there were—there were some teenage boys, but all those who spoke were middle-aged or old. Little Bear spoke in between. With-out raising his voice or sounding as if he were arguing, he seemed to be answering them, telling them what had to be done.

At the end of the talking, there was a long silence.

Omri thought: *They've accepted it.* Then an old man with snow-white hair stood up, clapped his hands, and raised them. He said a few words. That seemed to bring the talking part of the gathering to a close.

People began to murmur excitedly among themselves, while some of the men and boys arranged themselves in two lines, facing each other across the fire. They took their drums onto their laps and began to beat them with short sticks. The small drums had a strange, plangent note, as if they had water in them. Other men shook their rattles rhythmically. They began to chant.

Most of the others stood up and began to dance in a circle around the fire. Omri had seen Little Bear dance, when they'd been together in Omri's time. But this was different. The sounds of the chanting and drumming, the stamp and shuffle of feet, the flicker of the firelight on their expressionless, resigned faces, was the saddest thing Omri had ever known.

Of course they were used to moving around, they had several dwelling places—he knew that. But it's one thing to move when you want to. Another to be driven away, far away—not knowing where you'll end up or what will happen to you on the journey; to leave a house you've built with your own hands, which is home and place of worship and meetinghouse and ancestral command, all in one—and not know if you'll ever build another.

Perhaps they would never dance like this again, never sound their drums, never chant these sacred songs. Settlers would come and build their homes on this land and grow different crops on these fields—not the Three Sisters: corn, beans, and squashes—and cut down the bright-leaved trees and the straight, strong pines, and take the Indians' places, and never think about them except to curse them and be glad they'd gone.

Omri put his face down on the rim of the basket. He didn't want to watch the dancing anymore. It seemed Little Bear felt the same, because Omri felt the basket turn 180 degrees away from the fire. He raised his head and glanced sideways at his father. He had tears on his cheeks. They caught the firelight like the children's eyes.

And suddenly Omri realized something. Little Bear had turned away from the fire. *And still firelight caught Omri's father's tears.*

In that split second, everything changed.

Little Bear stiffened. Omri felt the jerk as his stomach muscles tightened against the back of the basket. Then he let out a great cry that pierced through the drumming and made it, and every other sound, stop. Then they could hear it. A roaring and crackling—and through the open door at the far end of the longhouse, they saw that smoke was *coming in*, and that beyond, the darkness was no longer dark.

"The stockade's on fire!" Omri's father shouted. "It's the settlers! They're attacking the longhouse!"

20

Murder

Little Bear dropped the basket.

Till now he'd been holding it cupped before him in his two hands, but now he let it go. It fell out of his hands as it fell out of his mind—Omri realized it later. At the time, there was only the horrible feeling of being in a lift whose cable suddenly snaps, that hurtles sickeningly toward the ground—no time to think, only time to feel terror.

But before the basket reached the ground, it was struck—kicked—sent flying again by running feet. Omri's father was pinning Omri to the side of the basket with an arm on either side. He was clutching the thick strands of plaited sweet grass, grimly holding on. The sturdy, springy weave of the basket cushioned some of the foot blows that landed against it, which perhaps also broke their fall. At one point they were rolling along the floor, flopping, lifting, dropping. Omri didn't notice when his *gustoweh* fell off. His gasps and cries went unheard in the mêlée going on above and all around them as the Indians, emitting yelps and shouts, rushed pell-mell toward the smoke-filled open doorway.

Omri lay on the earth floor with the breath knocked out of him. His father was half on top of him. The basket lay over them, a dark dome letting through little chinks and flashes of firelight.

"Are you okay?"

"I don't know."

"Can you move everything?"

Omri tried. His arms and legs worked, but his neck and shoulder hurt badly. "I think I've wrenched my neck."

His father stood up. One leg nearly gave way under him, but he managed to heave the basket up and away. They were still in the longhouse, but much farther from the fire. The running feet must have kicked them halfway to the doorway.

They stared. Through the doorway they could see the tall, abutting posts of the palisade blazing. They could see the silhouettes of Indians, running, leaping—right *through* the flames! They saw raised tomahawks and heard their war cries. Dogs barked. Then there were shots. And all the time the sinister crackle and roar of the fire.

"What can we do? How can we help?" Omri suddenly shouted.

"We can't. We can't do a single damn thing," said his father between his teeth.

They heard sounds behind them, and turned. They saw that not everyone in the group around the fire had run outside. Many of the women had remained behind.

With frantic, fearful haste they were gathering up the younger children.

"They shouldn't stay here. They have to get out," said Omri's father. "They must—"

A tremendous crash behind them made them turn again. A section of the burning stockade had fallen inward, toward the longhouse, onto its roof. A mass of burning poles fell through the doorway and crashed to the ground in a wild uprush of sparks. A monstrous tidal wave of smoke five times their height rolled toward them and engulfed them, forcing them to turn and run the other way, back toward the central fire, coughing and choking, their arms over their eyes.

Suddenly Omri felt his father grab him.

"Wait!" he coughed. "Where's Tall Bear?"

"They left him—asleep—in the room—"

"We must get him!"

Had his father forgotten they were small? But they ran, as hard as they could despite their bruises and strained muscles. Omri knew which was Little Bear's compartment by now, it was the one with the short logs of elm and sweet-smelling pile of grass near it, Bright Stars's basket makings. To them it was about a hundred yards away. Eventually, they reached it and dived under the corn-husk curtain.

The room was relatively smoke-free so far. They could see Tall Bear amid the hides. He'd woken up and was sitting looking about him, a bewildered giant's child with black hair on end. When he saw them, his face broke into a smile. He went onto all fours and began to crawl eagerly toward them.

"Come on, Om—run—draw him after us!"

They dived back under the curtain and burrowed under the sweetgrass. Tall Bear crawled after them,

sticking his head out from under the curtain and looking around in the fire-lit darkness. Then he got a lung-
ful of smoke, and did exactly what Omri's dad had been
hoping. He let out a howl that turned into a noisy burst
of coughing.

Beside the fire, a woman's attention was caught. She
saw the baby and ran toward him, scooping him up in
her arms and carrying him away. The last they saw of
him, he was hanging over her shoulder, reaching out
his chubby hands toward them, yelling blue murder.

The wave of smoke had cleared a little, and wasn't so
thick down near the ground, where they were. Omri
could look around him.

"Where's Clan Mother?" he asked suddenly.

"There she is. She's still by the fire. They must have
forgotten her."

"We must do the dream!"

"What?"

But Omri couldn't wait to explain. He was running.
His shoulder and neck hurt fearfully, but it was as if
the pain were somewhere else. It didn't stop him. He
ran as hard as he could, and his father came limping
behind him with one stiff knee, gasping "What? What
are you doing?" Omri ran on ahead, trusting his dad to
follow as best he could.

It was a long way to the fire, and to the old woman.
By the time he got there, Omri was practically exhausted, and his lungs and eyes were protesting bitterly
against the smoke. He thought frantically, *Her eyes! She
looks half blind! She probably won't even see us through
all this!*

But when he came up to her and tugged the skirt
near her folded knee, and shouted and waved his arms,
she looked down slowly, as if she had been in a trance,

and then sharply bent closer. She saw him! She reached out her hand to catch hold of him. But this wasn't what he wanted.

He dodged and ran a little distance away. He turned. Her eyes had followed him. He was on the far side of her now. He remembered how the Indian had said the little person in her dream behaved. He stood still, out of her reach, and pointed toward the far doorway, the one without the fire, and beckoned strongly with his other arm.

He heard her give a gasp. And then at once, she started to lever herself to her feet.

A passing woman noticed her struggles to get up and helped to lift her. The clan mother clutched her with both hands, shouting at her, pointing to the nearest doorway, through which could be seen nothing but darkness—the stockade fire had not yet crept right round to the other side. The woman nodded and ran off.

"She's gone to call the others!" Omri said to his father, who had just stumbled up to him. "They'll take their kids and go out through the far door!"

"But how will they get through the stockade? The only gap is at the other end!"

Omri stood stock-still. He hadn't thought of that. Surely the raiders wouldn't have wanted the women and children to be trapped in the burning longhouse? That would be too wicked.

Women were now mustering, keeping their children close. They seemed well organized; there was no panic. The smoke from the burning at the far end was thickening, and many of the children were coughing, though not many were crying. Omri remembered that Indian children were taught not to cry. He looked back. The flaming poles that had fallen had set light to the dry bark of the end wall. That end of the longhouse was already well alight.

Suddenly he felt the skin on the right side of his face begin to prickle and quiver. It was remembering, the way parts of the body can, the injury it had got the last time he'd gone back in time. His face was afraid—afraid of being burnt again. This fear communicated itself to the rest of him and he felt suddenly weak and helpless. Abruptly, he was so overtaken with fear he could hardly speak.

"Dad! Let's get out of here—please!"

"Get to the side of the aisle, or we'll be kicked again."

They ran to the side, stood against an upright pole, and then turned. The small crowd of women and children were starting to move swiftly toward the empty black-dark doorway at the end away from the blaze.

But suddenly it wasn't empty anymore.

Two men—not Indians—appeared in it. One held a flaming torch in one hand and a flintlock pistol in the other. The other cradled a musket.

The women stopped dead.

There was a long, horrible moment when nobody moved. There must have been sounds coming from the other end of the longhouse, but it was as if Omri's ears went dead. The moment caught and held and was full of utterly silent menace. He had time to notice that the men were smiling—grinning at the crowd of women, as if getting ready to greet them.

Then there was panic. The women, many still clutching children in their arms or dragging them by the hand, turned and fled down the aisle. The central fire partly blocked their escape route, and one woman, running blindly, tripped and fell into the glowing embers. She screamed. Her little boy screamed, too, and pulled her by the arm as she struggled to roll clear of the smoldering logs. Then there was a bang that nearly stopped Omri's heart.

The woman seemed to lift off the ground, and then fell back, motionless, her head in the embers. Her hair began to burn, but she didn't move. Her little son stood there, frozen, gaping. The whole thing took about a second. Then another shot rang out, a deeper, roaring sound, and after a brief pause for reloading, the flintlock fired again, through the smoke toward the fleeing backs.

Omri couldn't believe what he was seeing. He just stood there watching, stunned with horror. He had forgotten his father, Little Bear, Clan Mother. All he could think of was Bright Stars. Was she among the fleeing women? Was she the one he saw leaving the ground as a shot hit her, and then dropping?

Then he realized something else. At the far end, they couldn't get out. They were trapped by the blaze. The settlers could just come around the central fire toward them and pick them off, one by one, at their leisure.

The only thing that was delaying this was the smoke.

The women, brought up short by the blaze, were doubling back, ducking into the compartments, hiding behind the corn-husk curtains. Omri saw one dodging into Little Bear's compartment. Was it Bright Stars? Where was she? Where was Tall Bear? He couldn't see! He couldn't see!

The men had lost sight of their targets. But they knew they had them, that there was no escape. They moved down the aisle quite calmly. One touched the torch to the bottoms of the corn-husks, which caught like the dry leaves they were, and the fire streamed up them. Soon the whole building would be ablaze and the women sheltering in those compartments would be—

A strong, hard hand closed around Omri and lifted him.

He gasped and struggled, but it was useless. He'd had both of the men in his sight—it wasn't them! Who had picked him up?

He twisted his head in breathless fear. It was Old Clan Mother! Why hadn't she run away with the other women? And he saw his father in her other hand. She was walking with them. Walking, not running. Not away from the men, but toward them.

21

Clan Mother's Courage

The men couldn't believe their eyes when they saw this old, old woman, half-hidden by smoke, with her long white hair and glittering, squinting eyes, walking slowly, with her arms stretched ahead of her like a blind person, marching into the muzzles of their guns. Blocking the way to their murderous purpose.

They stopped in their tracks. The grins fell off their bearded faces. Their gun arms slackened uncertainly. Then one of the men raised his pistol and pointed it at her.

"Keep back, ye crazy old heathen!" he barked. But his voice shook.

She kept coming, and the other man shrank and backed away.

And suddenly she emerged from the wreathing smoke into the circle of bright light from the flaming torch. Now they could see clearly what was in the hands she was holding out in front of her.

Omri, half-paralyzed with terror though he was, realized what she was doing.

The Indians might believe in and accept little people. But not these men. Clan Mother had seen enough of white men to know that.

In a split-second memory, he recalled Mr. Johnson, his old headmaster, who had once seen Omri's own little people and had thought he had lost his mind. He remembered Patrick's story about the saloon bar in old Texas—the drunks who had seen him, a tiny human, and run away in terror.

But one of them had shot at him first. Now Omri—and his dad—were in the line of fire.

He never knew afterward if it was abject terror or cleverness that made him begin to shout and scream, imitating the Indians' war cries. Whether his wild gestures were struggles to escape, or what the men perceived—threats and defiance from some tiny supernatural being.

Omri was almost level with the men's faces—he saw them freeze into masks of terror. As the old woman kept relentlessly shuffling closer, they backed and backed. . . . The one who had not spoken suddenly let out an inarticulate shout. His musket dropped from his nerveless hands, and he turned and fled into the night.

The other one was left alone. He tensed, crouched, caught between two impulses. He looked wild, terrified, like a cornered animal. His pistol, recently reloaded, was still aimed. His hand was shaking wildly, but at this range he couldn't miss.

The old woman thrust her hands even farther forward and shook them almost into the settler's face. Omri could smell the mustiness of his beard, whiskey on his breath, the sour sweat of fear coming off him. Omri's throat seized up. He couldn't force out another sound.

In one more second he would be looking straight into the barrel of that enormous death-dealing weapon.

But Old Clan Mother had a last tactic up her sleeve.

She dropped the arm that held Omri. The gun, pointed at her face, was level. It steadied. And then that withered arm made one last, heroic, wholly unlooked-for effort. It jerked straight up, and Omri felt the barrel of the pistol strike his shoulder sharp and hard. The gun, as it was struck, fired, nearly deafening him, but the ball went high, into the roof.

The man's nerve broke, and he ran, dropping pistol and torch. *They've gone, we're safe!* flashed through Omri's fear-drenched brain. But suddenly the man stopped and snatched up the discarded musket. As he was about to disappear through the doorway, he paused for one moment, and turned back.

"Go back to hell, ye red devil!" he yelled hoarsely and fired one last thunderous shot.

The old woman stiffened. Her grasp on Omri loosened. Instinctively he wrapped his arms around one of her gnarled fingers. Then he was arcing through the air as she crashed backward to the ground.

The next few minutes passed in a kaleidoscope of confusion. The women and children came crowding round, and it was like being trapped in a forest of living trees. . . . There were wails and cries of grief. The old woman, who was now a huge motionless mountain in whose flickering shadow Omri and his father crouched, was lifted and carried away.

They should have stayed in the open, where they could be seen and perhaps rescued, but their instincts were too strong. Like exposed mice they fled from the trampling moccasins and the smoke and noise and danger into the nearest compartment. Scrambling over a heap of furs and other objects, they mounted the sleeping platform, still smelling sweetly and innocently of its sage mattress.

They only spoke a few brief, panting words to each other.

"That wasn't Bright Stars, before—the one who—?"

"No."

"Where did she go?"

"Out with the men. Don't talk. Help me make a hole in one of these slabs of bark."

His dad stared around the football field of a bed, and saw something glint. It was a knife, almost as big as himself. Omri watched as he ran to it, stumbling and tripping over the huge folds of hide, and picked it up, dragged it back, and began struggling to pierce one of the bark shingles in the outer wall. In the end he got Omri to help him and they used it like a battering ram. Between them they pierced and twisted a hole in the bark, big enough to enable them to squeeze through and climb down the ten feet or so to the ground. Omri would have fallen if his father had not been below to catch him.

"Come on, we can't stay here. We've got to get away from the longhouse."

They ran through the flickering darkness, but after about two hundred yards, they were brought up short by a huge barrier. It was the stockade.

"The fire hasn't got to this part yet! We've got to get through!"

They examined it as well as they could in the dark. It had been all too well constructed, the stripped tree trunks so close together that a beetle couldn't have squeezed between them, and above them the sharpened tops were invisible—twice as high as the longhouse roof and now lost in smoke and darkness. It stretched interminably away on either side.

Which way to run? Neither of them had the least idea, and both were disoriented by fear and exhaustion. They had both been hurt, and their injuries, though not serious themselves, had begun to stiffen and give real pain. The numbness where the pistol barrel had struck Omri's shoulder now began to feel red-hot, and he saw his dad rubbing his knee and grimacing.

"Dad—couldn't we just—sit here and wait—wait for Patrick? I don't think I can run anymore."

"I don't know what else we can do. . . . But if the longhouse collapses on us—"

They sank down, breathing heavily, at the foot of one of the poles. They could feel the heat, and hear the sound of burning, getting closer.

"How do you think those awful men got in?"

"They must have been inside the stockade already, before the fire was started."

"I suppose Little Bear's just forgotten about us," Omri said.

"I wouldn't blame him. I just hope he's all right. Do you think they managed to drive the raiders off? I heard shots—I mean from outside."

"That must have been the raiders. Little Bear said the Indians had no more bullets."

"They had their bows and arrows. I hope they got those swine! They purposely set out to trap the women inside the stockade."

After a few moments, Omri sat up straight. "Dad!"
"What?"

"They were! They are—they're trapped! The women I mean. The opening to the stockade is the part that's burning! I think the men jumped through when it was just starting, but all the women and kids must be still caught inside the stockade, the same as us!"

"Where?"

"They must be at the end, near the other door!"

Suddenly, through the roaring noise of the fire, came another sound.

Thwok-thwock-thwock.

"What's that!"

"I know! Quick—run toward it!"

They ran to their right. And now Omri could identify the sound—the most welcome sound possible at that dire moment.

The thudding of axes against wood.

"It's them! It's the men outside the stockade! They're using their trade axes to chop a hole to let everyone out!"

They ran, keeping close to the poles, around a bend near the corner of the longhouse. There, sure enough, they saw the crowd of women and children, huddled together. The sound of the chopping became frenzied—there didn't seem to be any time between blows. They could see which poles were being attacked because they quivered and shook. And very soon the first of them swayed and screeched and fell outward, leaving a long, trunk-shaped oblong through which they could see the night and a section of a man's figure, wielding a large axe with a metal blade.

Two minutes later the adjacent pole fell, and then the next. It was enough. The children could now be handed out, the women squeezing through after them. There was no panic now; the evacuation happened in a calm, orderly way. Bundles and baskets were pushed through. Some women were still running to and from the doomed longhouse, rescuing possessions and supplies.

At last the bodies were passed through—three of them. Men's arms received them, and there was a stunned silence broken by muted cries of anguish, sorrow, and rage.

Then, quite abruptly, everyone was through and Omri and his father were alone.

"Okay, come on. We have to get ourselves out now."

The posts had been cut at about twice Omri's father's height. It was still no easy matter for them to climb out, especially weakened and weary as they were.

"You go first, bub." And his father made Omri clamber onto his shoulders. Then, when he still couldn't reach, his dad took his feet in his hands and, straining, heaved him up to half the length of his arms till Omri could get a good grip on the shattered top of the stump and haul himself up with the soles of his moccasins pressed against the pole. His shoulder gave him hell, but he did it because he had to. But how was his dad to follow?

Omri stood on the top of the stump, surveying the scene beyond. It had seemed very dark at first beyond the stockade, where the light of the fire couldn't reach, but now he could see quite well, and he realized there was a brilliant three-quarters moon; it had only seemed dark before because they had been in the stockade's shadow.

Omri could see the whole group of Indians at a distance. He couldn't make out exactly what they were doing. Suddenly he saw a man on horseback and his spirits swooped up.

"Dad! Dad! I can see Little Bear!" he called to his father, still down below, above the increasing roar of the flames. "He'll see me, he'll get you out! And—wow!— Bright Stars is with him! They've got Tall Bear, they're all safe! Little Bear!" he shouted at the top of his voice. "Little Bear! We're here! Help!"

And he waved his arms and danced on the stump.

But Little Bear took no notice. He couldn't hear him. He was at the far side of the group. Omri could see him, gesturing, calling, neck-reining the pony in and out of the crowd. He seemed to be organizing them. He had a couple of muskets slung across his back and Omri knew he must have taken them off dead raiders. He wondered fleetingly if he'd had time to take any more scalps.

From the pony's back, he could probably have seen Omri, silhouetted against the flame-lit smoke, if only he would look in the right direction. But now he jumped down and was lost among the crowd, and then in the moonlight Omri saw an old woman being heaved onto the pony's back, followed by an old man who straddled the horse's flanks behind her. Then a bundle. . . . And with a sudden sickening of the heart, Omri realized.

They were leaving.

Now, tonight. Of course, what else? Their home was burning; most of their possessions, and what little safety they had had, were gone. What else could they do but to start their long, dangerous journey north tonight?

In fact they were moving off. Omri could just make out Bright Stars, with the baby on her back, leading the pony at the head of a straggling column. They were going . . . leaving Omri's dad trapped below and both of them stranded.

But that wasn't the worst. They were going without saying good-bye. Omri felt suddenly absolutely certain that he would never see Little Bear again, if Little Bear didn't see him now.

And how could he see him, when his back must be turned like everyone else's and he was heading away from the longhouse, up the hill, and into the dark wood?

22

A Sacred Object

As Omri stood on the stump, the fire hot on his back, feeling absolutely gutted, something came between him and the heat.

He swung round toward the longhouse, and saw a vast black looming figure. The next second it had seized him.

"Gotcha, ya varmint!"

Omri nearly passed out. It was one of the men who had tried to murder the women and children! He, too, must have been trapped. He had hidden while the Indians were there, while the women were escaping, and now he—and the other, Omri could see him, too—were going to creep away through the only way out.

"Where's th'other of 'em?"

A slight pause, then: "There! Where ya feet is! Watch out, he's a-tryin' to run!"

"Oh no ye don't!"

In another moment, Omri's dad had been pounced on and lifted in a coarse and filthy fist. The men stared at their captives, then at each other. Their faces wore wolfish grins. The one who held Omri squeezed him so hard he screamed.

"They's real as you or me! They ain't nothin' to be scared of! Try how yours squeaks when ya pinches him!" The other one twisted Omri's father's arm and gave a shout of glee.

"Stop! Don't!" shouted Omri.

The men burst out laughing. "Stop! Don't!" they cried in high, mocking voices. "They ain't nuthin'! They're more scareder'n we was!"

"They stopped us shootin' them Injun sows! Let's kill 'em. I c'd bite the head off of mine an' spit it half a mile!"

"Half a mile? Let's see ya!"

"Watch me." And he opened his cavernous whiskey-stinking mouth and made to put Omri's head in.

It was the end. Omri was sure of it. He was too exhausted to fight and there was no hope at all. In that split second, he gave himself up to a horrible death.

Something huge and heavy whistled past Omri and buried itself in the man's head.

He dropped like a stone, and Omri with him, but he had a soft landing on the man's stomach. A moment later his father dropped out of nowhere and landed beside him.

They looked up and saw the second man take a flying leap over the cut ends of the poles, and then they heard a faint, brief whistle. The arrow caught him in the chest and he seemed to pause in midair before crashing to the ground beyond the palisade.

Little Bear came straight to the gap in the poles. He saw Omri and his father on the chest of the dead man, and they saw him smile a little. He stepped over the stumps, picked them both up, stuck them into his belt. Then, without a word, he charged straight into the burning longhouse!

Omri and his father, already half stunned with shock, could only cover their noses and mouths with their hands, but it didn't help much. They choked and coughed and their eyes ran.

Omri tried not to breathe. His eyes were tightly closed. He didn't see where Little Bear was going. He felt the heat getting worse. He saw bright red through his eyelids. He smelt hair singeing—was it his? He cowered down in remembered terror—the fire! The fire!

He felt Little Bear stoop, half squashing them at his waist, then straighten, turn, and run—run—then a leap! Then the cold night air, blissfully smoke-free, caressed their faces and enabled them to open their smarting eyes.

They were at the palisade, where the two dead men lay, one inside, one out. The one whose skull had been split by the tomahawk was staring up at them through a veil of his own blood. The other lay on his face, the arrow broken under him. Little Bear put his foot on the first man's chest and wrenched out his weapon.

And then they heard the crash as the rooftree of the longhouse broke and the blazing building, from which they had just emerged, collapsed in a mighty surge of smoke and sparks that topped even the sharpened spikes on the stockade posts.

Little Bear leapt the stumps and ran a little way up-hill, stopped, turned, and looked back.

"Little Bear?"

The Indian's hand closed round Omri and lifted him level with his face. He was breathing hard.

"Forgive me," he said in his deep voice. "I forget you at time I fight. I forget you at time we leave. But our women tell me your action. You are no boy. You are warrior. You are my blood brother. Little Bear will not forget you again."

He set them on the ground and knelt before them. He laid something wrapped in skins between them.

"You will go back soon?" he asked.

"Tomorrow morning."

Little Bear hesitated, then took off one of his moccasins and laid it on the ground near them. It formed a sort of cave.

"No, Little Bear! You can't march barefoot!" exclaimed Omri's dad.

"Cold can kill *you*, not me," the Indian said. "You must not die. Bright Stars will make other moccasin, on journey." Then he said, "Now you will know why I came back."

He put his hands on the thing he had been carrying. It was flat and wrapped in buckskin, on which Omri could see beautiful decorations, colorless in the moonlight. But one whole corner was blackened by fire.

Little Bear was very still. He looked as if he were praying.

"This is holy," he said.

Reverently he unwrapped something oval and flat, and held it before his face. Omri gasped. It changed him—made him into another being, awesome, grotesque—an otherworldly stranger.

"False face hold spirit of ancestor," Little Bear said from behind the mask. "His voice called to me from the fire."

Omri's father was astonished. "Why are you showing

it to us, Little Bear? Isn't it only for your *sachems*—your holy people?"

Little Bear said, "Little Bear shows you this because you helped to save our women. You came with me to save the false face from great danger. You are not like other white men. Spirit in false face wishes you to have this great honor. Old Clan Mother—" He paused, but only for a split second, and his face showed no emotion. "She wish that I do this to show respect for little people of her dream."

He put the mask back into the buckskin bag. "He goes with us. Without him, no hope. No—" He clasped his hands, one set of fingers holding the other.

"Link—"

"Yes. Chain. Like Covenant Chain of Iroquois that holds tribes together, holds my people to the time before. Where we go now, we will be new, like babies, but born from nothing. Our ancestors must come with us."

"Yes," said Omri's father. "They're your history."

Omri was suddenly choked with feeling. He had the strangest impulse. He wanted to say words he knew in his heart he didn't mean, but the need was so strong he could hardly resist. He wanted to say, to beg: "Little Bear, take us with you!" At that moment he could have said good-bye to his whole life, so as not to have to say good-bye to him.

But he kept silent. He put out his hand and Little Bear bent and touched it with his finger where once their blood had mingled. They looked into each other's eyes and Omri knew, without knowing how he knew, that it was for the last time.

"We are of one mind," the Indian said.

And he rose, and turned, and ran, swift as a deer, up the hill and into the forest after his people.

* * *

Omri and his father lay out in the open all night.

Even huddled in the moccasin, it was bitterly cold and they felt they might not survive. They could hear wolves howling up in the woods. Once an owl swooped low over them, its white underparts flickering in the moonlight. They clung together, shivering and scared and almost unbearably lonely, now that Little Bear had gone.

Ironically, it was probably only the fact that the rest of the stockade—the part nearest to them—suddenly blazed up some time after midnight, that saved them from the effects of the frost and from marauding animals.

In the deepest, darkest part of the night, when his dad was dozing, Omri cried. He put head and shoulders out of the moccasin cave and looked down the hill at the longhouse. There was little left. Each time small gusts of wind blew on it, its embers glowed fitfully like some dying thing drawing its last painful breaths. Omri cried bitter silent tears of sadness for his Indian and what he had left behind, and for Omri's loss of him.

Just as the sky was paling and Omri could see the streaks of clouds to the east, showing the blackened, still-smoking longhouse and the abandoned fields beyond, it all ended.

Omri didn't even have time to savor one final second. Only, as he traveled faster than light through the layers of time, the smell of the smoked hide and the burnt wood and the unsullied earth they were lying on—and a strange, vagrant whiff of sweetgrass—stayed with him in his nostrils even after he got home.

23

Patrick's Bit of Fun

"*I* *do remember well where I should be, and there I am.*"

These were the first words Omri heard when he opened his eyes, and it was to be a long time before he heard them again. When he did, he remembered them and realized that his father, in his shocked, dazed state, had said a line from Shakespeare.

It didn't sound strange at the time; it sounded quite right. They *were* where they should be: sitting in the car on Peacock Hill, looking through the windscreen at the sun (which was five hours' travel higher than it had been a split second ago). And for several moments that was all they did.

Then Omri remembered he had hurt his shoulder and moved it; the pain was still there. He thought of the ogre, squeezing his ribs, and breathed deep and felt it. He remembered he'd been wearing buckskin leggings and moccasins and a breechcloth, but now he was dressed in ordinary clothes. He remembered that, before he'd left, he had been sitting on a pile of sleeping bags and had his feet on a box. But those had gone.

"They must have been burnt in the fire," he murmured, frowning. Then he turned his head slowly to the right and saw Patrick.

He was on the driver's side of the car, standing outside the window, looking in at them. His face looked funny. Omri couldn't say how. Red, as if he'd been running, rather shiny. His mouth was open.

"Hi, Patrick," Omri said.

Patrick didn't answer. He was scrambling into the back of the car.

"Get home," he said. "Quick."

Now Omri's dad seemed to wake up. He twisted his head over his shoulder, and winced. "What's the rush?"

"I'll try to tell you as we go," said Patrick. Omri stiffened. He sounded as if he'd been crying. *Patrick? Crying?* "Please, please hurry!"

The key was in the ignition—of course. Patrick had just turned it. Slowly, as if he were stiff and aching, Omri's dad took the spare key out of the glove compartment and used it to start the engine.

"I remember now. I'll have to back all the way down. Damn."

"Shall I walk behind the car, Dad, and guide you?"

"Don't bother, I can manage."

And he did, more or less. But it was too tense for talking. Several times he ran the back wheels up the side of the narrow track and had to edge forward again, and once they thought they'd got stuck in the sand— the wheels spun maddeningly. Patrick, in a fever of impatience, jumped out and hurled himself against the bonnet, and got them clear.

And then they were back on the road, and Omri, deeply uneasy, said to Patrick, "Why do we have to hurry?"

"I've—I've lost Boone."

Omri twisted his head, ricking his neck. "Lost him? What do you mean? Lost him?"

"And Ruby Lou. I—I brought them back. I—they—I thought it'd be fun to give them a boat ride. I found your old coracle—you know, that miniature boat thing you got in Wales. It was a bit big for them but it floated beautifully, and I filled the bath up and—and put them in the coracle and showed them how to row. I made special little oars for them out of ice cream spoons—the real oar was too big—"

"Wait a minute. Did they want to do this, or was it your idea?"

"Never *mind* that now! I'm telling you! They got the idea and they were rowing around in the bath and *enjoying themselves*, and then your mum called me for breakfast. I meant to go back straight afterward, but there was this program Gillon was watching on TV, and—"

By this time Omri was kneeling up on the front seat and gazing over the back of it at Patrick in growing anxiety.

"You forgot them!"

"Your mum must've gone into the bathroom and seen the bath was full and just—pulled the plug."

"Did she see them?"

"Couldn't have done. She'd have said something."

"So the water ran out. *So what?*"

"So . . . I went back, and—the coracle was there in the bottom of the bath, and—and—"

Omri just stared at him. He wasn't breathing. Something awful was coming.

"And they were gone. Both of them."

"Where? How could they be gone?"

"I don't know. But Kitsa had been there."

Omri gasped. His father swerved the car into the side of the road—they were about a hundred yards from home—and turned toward Patrick.

"You don't mean the cat had—"

"Where? Where was she?"

"She'd gone back to her kittens. But she'd been in the bath. I could see her paw marks."

There was a terrible silence in the car. Then Omri's father slowly turned round and drove on. What was there to say? There was nothing to say. All Omri could do was sit there trying not to see in his mind's eye what he was seeing.

"You left them in the bathroom. All alone. You left the door open—"

"No! Of course I didn't! I shut it, I'm certain I did, but your mum left it open."

"You left them there for anybody to find—"

"There was just the three of us and we were all downstairs eating."

Eating. . . . Omri said suddenly, "Stop the car, Dad." But it was too late. He threw up, mostly out of the window. Then he just hung there, breathless and sweating, thinking, *Not Boone. Not Boone. Not Ruby. No.* He wanted to hit Patrick, he wanted to murder him. No, he didn't. He just wanted to be back in time, two hundred years before this awful thing had happened.

Twenty minutes ago, it hadn't happened, the sun was just coming up. . . .

He pulled his head in and said hollowly, "When did it—?"

"Just now. This morning. Just before I had to leave to get you back. I ran the whole two miles. Uphill."

Omri's imagination was out of control. He could see Boone and Ruby, trapped in the vast slippery wet whiteness of the bath, running frantically, trying uselessly to climb the sheer sides, with the great monster behind them. He saw Kitsa, an innocent but deadly pawn to her killer instincts, dabbing at them with lightning claws. . . . He saw Ruby, the lace of her white wedding dress snagged on those claws, being hooked into that waiting mouth. He remembered his own near-fate in the mouth of the settler.

It was too hideous! He should never, never have left Patrick alone with that key!

He became aware of the utter stillness of his father beside him.

"Was the coracle upside down? Could they have turned it over and hidden under it?"

Patrick shook his head. "It was upside down, but I looked."

"Where? Whereabouts in the bath?"

Despairingly, Patrick mumbled, "I tell you they're gone."

"*Where was it?*" Omri's father suddenly roared.

"Right over the plug-hole."

"AH!"

In a flash, he was out of the car, with Omri, bewildered but suddenly with a pinprick of hope, after him. Moving as fast as his bad knee would let him, his father hobbled up the path and into the house. He brushed aside Omri's mother, who had heard the car and was coming to meet them, and struggled up the stairs at the front-door end. Omri and Patrick came after him; in fact at the top Patrick dodged ahead. By the time the other two reached the bathroom, Patrick was already hanging over the tap end of the bath, trying to poke his fingers down the drain.

"Is it big enough? Could they have gone down there to save themselves?"

"Easily."

The drainpipe was old, like everything else in the cottage. It was open. It didn't have the usual metal fitting in its opening to stop things going down. But Omri's father picked something up. It was a little round metal thing like a tea strainer.

"Your mother always puts this in the mouth of the drain when she lets water out," he said. "To stop hairs and things blocking it. But, see, it's been moved." He picked up the coracle, a round black toy boat about five inches across made of wicker with an oilskin cover and a wooden seat. He looked at the boys. Hope was stark on his face.

"My bet is, Boone got himself and Ruby under the upturned coracle, and edged it down the bath until he was over the drain. Then they moved this strainer out of the way, and down they went. Fell, or jumped."

Patrick looked as if his knees might collapse under him.

"You mean, they might not be dead?"

"I mean they might have escaped from Kitsa. But if they did go down there, they could easily have drowned."

"Lionel?"

They all spun round. Omri's mother was standing in the doorway, a look of hurt bewilderment on her face.

"I thought you were rushing up here like a madman

because you needed to *go*. Don't I get even a hallo after two days?"

Omri's father and Omri rushed to hug her.

"Sorry, Mum—it was just—" But of course he couldn't explain. Omri's dad leapt into the breach.

"Patrick told us he'd dropped his—er—"

"My *watch*—"

"Ah, yes, down the drain. He's terribly upset. Sorry, darling." He gave his wife a contrite kiss.

"Well. Okay. So how did it go?"

Omri's dad looked into her face, and then looked away. Omri got some faint inkling of how extremely difficult it is for happily married people to keep secrets from each other.

"It was . . . it was . . ." he said with a helpless air.

"It was absolutely fabulous, Mum," said Omri.

His mother gave a big, bland smile.

"I want to know *everything*," she said, "every tiny detail. Come on down. Why are you limping?"

"We—we had a bit of a fall. In the mist. It's nothing."

"Oh, good. As to Patrick's watch—how could you possibly drop it down there? I put the strainer in, I know I did."

There was a silence. Then she sighed and said, "Boys . . . I don't know. Come on, then," and went out.

"What'll we do?" whispered Patrick.

"First thing," Omri's dad whispered back, "you must call down there and see if they answer. Then drop a weighted string down and see how deep it is. After that—" He shrugged. "I'm sorry. I have to go." And he limped out, leaving the boys alone.

*   *   *

They called down. Nothing. They dropped a string weighted with a toothbrush. It went down about a foot and then stopped where the pipe bent.

"There's one good thing," Omri said. "The water goes down very slowly. Mum's always complaining about it. If they jumped they would have landed in the water in the pipe and it would have carried them down the pipe quite gently."

"*If* they could swim."

"Or were clinging on to the paddles you made."

The boys went to the window. They could see the pipe running down the outside corner past the kitchen. There was an open drain with a grating down there.

"Maybe they're there—maybe the grating caught them!"

They raced downstairs and round to the back. But there was nothing on the grating. It had big spaces between the bars, through which two tiny people could easily have been washed by a downflow of water.

"Then what? Where would they go? Into the big drain?"

"We're not on mains drainage," said Omri. "All our wastewater goes into—Oh, NO!"

Leaving Patrick to follow, Omri raced back into the house. His father was in the kitchen with his mother, who was just handing him a mug of coffee.

"Dad! The septic tank!"

Omri had no time to think about avoiding involving his mother. All he could think of was Boone and Ruby Lou in the ghastly sewer tank under the flower bed in the front garden. Nothing mattered except getting them out. *If* they were in there. *If* they were still alive, not devoured or drowned or asphyxiated or frightened to death down there in the vast echoing smelly darkness.

His father literally dropped the mug of coffee, which shattered on the tiles. He grabbed his wife by the shoulders.

"Stay here," he said. "Don't come out!"

Then he was bolting past the boys, through the front part of the house and out into the front garden.

At the edge of the central flower bed, he halted. "A crowbar!" he shouted. "Omri! Fetch that iron rod I clean the culvert with!"

For a moment Omri's mind was a blank. Then he remembered seeing it across the lane in one of the bays. When he returned with it about ten seconds later, he found his father and Patrick struggling to lift the heavy manhole cover with their hands. They could barely shift it.

Omri's father snatched the rod out of Omri's hands and applied it to a special slot in the lid. It was like lifting a huge, heavy stove lid. Omri watched helplessly, remembering that it had taken two men to lift it when they'd come to empty the tank. He drew in a sharp breath. They'd emptied the tank! Quite recently! At least it wouldn't be full. And there were the little bugs down there, reducing the "solids" (ugh!) to harmless sludge. And the water drained away all the time. Maybe they wouldn't drown, if they'd got that far through the pipes safely.

His father strained and gave it his full strength. And the lid moved! As soon as it came off, the boys fell on their knees on the earth and put their heads into the manhole.

"Boone! Ruby! Are you in there?" And Patrick added between desperately clenched teeth, "Oh, please! Be in there!"

Their voices echoed emptily round the inside of the tank.

24

Visitors

For long seconds, the echo of their own voices was all that came back to them, and the dark shadow of despair threatened them again.

And then, amplified by the awful depths, they heard a well-known Texan voice.

"If thet's you, Patrick, Ah wouldn't advise ya to git us outta here. If'n Ah wuz you, Ah'd leave us here ter *rot*. Because if'n Ah ever git out, Ah'm a gonna bust yor nose wide open. Ah'm gonna kick yor big ornery butt. Ah'm gonna shove that thur boat o' yorn right down yer mizzable throat. An' *then,* when Ah done all thet, Ah'm gonna shoot ya full a lead, right through the belly button!"

"Oh, Boone! Oh, Boone!" was all Patrick could say, grinning through tears of joy, as if the prospect of being busted, kicked, choked, and shot by his cowboy was all he could wish for, world without end.

The next moment he had practically dived headfirst into the tank. Omri and his dad had to catch hold of his feet to stop him falling right in. A moment later a hollow shout from within told them to drag him back out.

He emerged, filthy to the elbows but triumphant. In each hand he held a tiny sludge-blackened figure.

Boone had somehow, incredibly, managed to keep jammed on his head his ten-gallon hat, which he now wrenched off, showing untainted red hair and a white crescent at the top of his filthy face. He took the hat by its brim in both hands and began to belabor Patrick's hand with it.

"Ah'll kill ya. That's what Ah'll do, ya varmint! Ah'll beat ya to death! Of all the stinkin'est places Ah ever bin in, an' Ah bin in plenty, that thur has gotta be the worst! Look at me! Ah smell like Ah fell in the privvy!"

"Well, as a matter of—"

"Don't you utter a dad-blamed word, ya mizzable no-count low-life kid, you!" His voice pitched up and went British, in a mockery of Patrick's. "Whay don't yew go a-boatin', Boone, yew'll love it, it's quite safe! *Boatin'*— who in hell that wuz ever born in the State o'Texas knows or cares anythin' about boats! Hosses—yep. Boats? No, sir! As fur water, Ah don't even like *drinkin'* the stuff! But Ah tried. Agin all that's decent and natural fur a Texan, Ah tried, jest t'please ya, but then what? Ya left us to make a meal fur thet gol-danged rotten cat that darn near killed me once awready! And as if thet wasn't enough, we had t'jump down a well and git ourselves half drownded, and then—"

While he raved, Omri removed the other figure from Patrick's hand. It was Ruby, of course. He held her gently and looked at her. She wasn't wearing her wed-

ding dress anymore. She was dressed for riding. Her beautiful blond hair was all filthy and wet and so were her clothes. But she didn't seem to notice. She was leaning out of Omri's hand, waving both arms at Boone and cheering him on.

"You tell him, Billy! You give it to him, lover! If you don't I will! Oooooh, if ever I miss havin' kids, I'll only have to think they mighta bin like that lousy snake-eyed Pat, that I thought was the greatest kid on earth, and I'll just thank m'lucky stars I ain't got none!"

"Ruby—"

"WHAT!"

"I think Patrick's really sorry."

"Sorry ain't enough for what we bin through!"

"Would you like to clean up?"

She seemed to notice Omri for the first time. She squinted up at him through the dirt, and her angry face softened.

"Well now, that's a purty darn silly question, I'd say."

"Come on. I'll take you."

As Omri turned toward the house, he thought he saw a face at the window nearest the door, but it vanished.

Omri and Patrick crept upstairs, to the bathroom, scene of the crime. Omri ran warm water into the coracle, which was about the size of a jacuzzi to Boone and Ruby. He put a drop of bubble bath in to make it smell nice, and cut a clean wash cloth into towels for them while Patrick carved a couple of chips off a cake of soap with some nail-scissors. They laid these on the wooden seat that spanned the circular coracle, and set a sort of screen around it made of two opened books (kept handy by the loo).

It was Patrick who thought of pouring a dribble of shampoo into a lid and lowering it into the new-made "bathroom" so Ruby Lou could wash her hair. At that, Omri, not to be outdone, found an old mascara brush of his mother's and washed it carefully so Boone could use it to scrub his back.

"You're going to have to have a good wash this time, Boone," he couldn't resist saying as he dropped it over the screen. He could already hear groans of pleasure as Ruby Lou lowered herself into the hot water.

His dad had had an even better idea. He arrived a few minutes later with the lid of a Chap Stick full of Scotch. He opened the "screen" a crack (to be greeted by a modest shriek from Ruby) and pushed it through.

"Drop of the hard stuff for you, Boone," he said.

"A *drop!*" screamed Ruby. "A bucketful, more like! You shouldn't encourage him. I just got done makin' him give it up again!" But the capful of whiskey was speedily dragged in, and they could hear appreciative gulps and lip smacks, and then they heard Ruby say, "Okay, buster, no need to hog it all, save a snifter fer Ruby—I need it as bad as you do!"

"Let's leave them in peace," Omri's dad whispered.

"What if Mum wants to come into the bathroom? Or Gillon?"

"Gillon's at a friend's. Mum's busy. Anyway, I'll stand guard."

The boys left the bathroom and heard the lock click into place. Omri said to Patrick, "He'd have done it, I bet. Everything he was threatening you with. If he'd just been big enough, you'd have been a goner."

"Wouldn't have blamed him," Patrick mumbled.

They went into Omri's room.

The first thing Omri saw as he walked in was a tiny black horse standing in a makeshift corral on his desk. But the next thing he saw made him stop in his tracks.

There beside the horse was a plastic bag. It was empty.
And then he saw four little plastic figures standing in
a row.

"Patrick—" he croaked out. "You didn't—"

"No. I nearly did. I *damn* nearly did."

Omri stared at him speechlessly.

"Listen, Om. You think Boone was mad. I was ten
times madder. No, now just listen. After you left, I spent
the day hiking and picnicking, and then I camped out
on the hill for the night as I said I would, and I was
just, like, *seething* the whole time. Then I came back
down here and fed your mum that line we agreed to. I
don't think she believed a word of it, but for some weird
reason she didn't argue. Then I had to settle down here
for a whole day yesterday, with nothing to do but think
of the fun you and your dad were having without me."

Fun . . . Omri dropped his eyes. "Go on."

"So last night I just couldn't stand it. I came in here
and started looking for where you'd hidden your little
people. It wasn't too hard, because you'd left fingerprints on the door and I could see they were soot. So I
looked up the chimney and I found them right away."

Omri scowled. So much for his brilliant hiding place.

"Well, I had the key, so I put them in the cupboard,
and I was going to do it—all of them—but then I
thought, no, one at a time was better, and I was going
to bring Little Bear first because I knew he was looking
after you. I wanted to. To take him away from you, kind
of. But I thought I'd just bring Matron first. Of course
she was no fun at all. She was so mad at me for inter-
rupting her work—she said a whole bunch of soldiers
wounded at a place called Dunkirk had just been
brought in and she had no time for children's games.
So I sent her back, quick.

"Then I brought Sergeant Fickits. He was okay. He sat and talked to me and told me about the army. It sounds really good; I might just join when I'm older—the Royal Marines, I mean, not the ordinary army. And I found myself telling him about you guys going off to the past without me and how I wanted to—well, to do something about it. Only Fickits was against it. He said, what about comradeship and team spirit, and what if something was going on—even if Little Bear was just carrying you when I brought him and he suddenly fell down, he might squash you, and if things were really going badly for the Indians there might be danger for you, too. Was there?" he asked eagerly. "Did you have a terrific adventure? What happened to your dad's leg?"

"I'm going to tell you everything. Just please finish your part."

"Well, like Fickits made me think about it a bit, like imagine what might be happening and how me sticking Little Bear in the cupboard might cause something worse to happen. So I just got Fickits something to eat—I wanted to open a can of beer for him but I knew your mum'd notice—and we ate together and talked some more and then he said he had to get back because of Suez. I said what's Suez and he told me I was an ignorant young git. But he was really nice otherwise, and you've got him to thank I didn't bring Little Bear after all."

"But you did bring Boone and Ruby Lou."

"Yeah. Well, they're mine. I couldn't see anything against that, and I was still mad and I wanted to have some fun. So I brought them, and we had a great time together. They told me what-all they'd been doing—"

"You're talking like him—"

"And how they'd opened a saloon and eating house.

Like, Ruby runs it and does the cooking and keeps the customers in order, sort of, and Boone did all the decorations, with paintings all over the walls, and folks come from miles around to see it. They used to call it just Ruby's Saloon, but now everyone calls it the Picture Palace. Isn't that funny? Think of all the places that'll be called that in a few years, because of movies! And Boone and Ruby's place is the first!"

"Was."

"Is, was—what's the difference? It's all just *happening*, isn't it?"

Omri nodded slowly. That was for sure.

"As soon as they've had a wash and got their clothes dry, we must send them back. They had to close the saloon for repairs after a bit of a fight at the bar, but they need to get back. Isn't it fantastic that it's all turned out okay?" he said with a carefree laugh, as if nothing at all bad had happened. "Let's go back to the bathroom and see how they're getting on."

And off he went. Omri heard him tapping on the door, and his father letting him in. But Omri stood for a moment looking at Matron, Fickits, Little Bear, and Bright Stars with Tall Bear in her arms, and thought: *I could bring them. I could.* But something inside him said *No. It's over.* Omri felt the heavy sadness again and pressed the argument, the simple argument: *But I could! I've got the cupboard. There's the key, stuck in its lock. I could!*

But it was like a brick wall inside him. He knew he mustn't. Couldn't.

Was this his magic part, the part his dad thought he'd inherited from Jessica Charlotte? Or was it just some instinctive wisdom, perhaps brought back with him from his time with the Indians, who knew things modern people had forgotten or never learnt?

Anyhow there was no gainsaying it.

He took the four little figures and packed them away carefully in the cashbox with Jessica Charlotte and the others. He closed the lid quietly, remembering how he had once tied string tightly round the Chinese boxes he'd kept his little people in, and buried them in box after box to make it hard to get at them. He didn't need to do that this time.

Because who would he be protecting it from? Only himself. And he didn't need to. He decided to give the key back to his mother. She could hang it on her medallion-chain, like before. This time he would never ask her to give it back to him. *I can trust myself now,* he thought.

EPILOGUE

Boone and Ruby went home, clean, shiny, rather drunk, and in a much more mellow mood.

"Ah fergive ya, son," Boone said to Patrick just before they left, and added, "Shucks, is it muh soft heart, or is it the whiskey talkin'?" Ruby even gave him a kiss. And a few hours later, Patrick himself, with his little people in his pocket, was put on the train.

He went off quite cheerfully, his mind afire with Omri's story, told to him faithfully throughout most of what had remained of their last day. He couldn't be entirely sorry he hadn't been there, but: "I'm going next time!" were his parting words. Omri said nothing. He couldn't possibly tell him yet that there would be no next time.

Omri and his dad longed to spend time together, mulling over all that had happened, but his dad said, "Not yet. I've neglected Mum, and I feel bad about it. I feel

bad altogether about shutting her out. . . . I think we
ought to try to get back to normal and not keep creeping
off together."

So life went on as before in the Dorset longhouse.
Gillon went back to school. Adiel came home for the
next weekend, and their mum cooked a proper Sunday
lunch. Omri thought she was a bit quieter than usual,
but he was so busy with his own thoughts and memories
he didn't pay her much attention.

And then one day, a week after their return, his
mother came into his bedroom without her usual knock
when he was doing his homework. He turned to see
what she wanted and caught a look on her face that he
had never seen there before.

"I think this probably belongs to a friend of yours,"
she said.

And she came to him with something between her
finger and thumb. She laid it carefully on his exercise
book. Then she went out again.

He didn't notice her leave. He was staring down at
the tiny thing she had laid there. It was so small that
nobody would have noticed it if they had not been looking for it. Less than an inch long and no wider than
string; but you could see the pattern on it if you peered
very closely.

The wampum belt.

He left it there with a glass of water on top of it
lest it blow away in the breeze from his window. And
went downstairs.

His mother was in the kitchen sorting laundry. She
was always banging on at them for leaving tissues and
other things in the pockets of clothes they threw in the
wash, and now she was going through the pockets her-

self. Omri's eyes went to the pile she'd already done and saw at once the shirt his father had been wearing the day they had set off.

He stood silently, and she knew he was there but for a long time she just went on working without a word. Then she said, "I suppose I'm never going to see them now."

And it burst on him like something exploding in his brain.

Of course. It was through his mother that he had inherited whatever he had of Jessica Charlotte's gift. She had some, too. She had seen the ghost. She knew things. *She knew about this.* She had known all the time. Or for ages, anyway.

He went up behind her and touched her arm.

She turned quickly and held him. "You're right," she said passionately, though he hadn't spoken. "It's too dangerous. I've been so frightened sometimes! I've been so frightened!" And she was crying.

"You knew—about Gillon's puppet dream?"

She nodded. "I still thought you were dead in the car, though."

"And before? My story about the Indian?"

"Yes. I couldn't let you know I knew. But now I can because it's going to stop. It has stopped. Hasn't it?"

"Yes."

"Thank God," she said.

How had she held it in? Pretended all this time that she didn't notice, didn't know? Let them treat her as if she were practically dim-witted? How had she let them do all that they'd done?

"You're wonderful, Mum," he said humbly.

"No. You shouldn't give me credit. It's something inside. I know *you* understand."

"Does Dad know you know?"

"No, but you can tell him. Don't tell the boys *any-thing*, though. Don't ever tell them. They'd never let it rest."

That night, when his dad came to his room to say good night to him, Omri showed him the belt.

"Where did you find it?"

"It was—it was in your shirt pocket."

"We must send it back."

"Couldn't we keep it?"

"Omri, no! You know what it is—it's got part of the history of the tribe woven into it. They need it, the way they need the false face. You know in the Bible when the Israelites were driven away from their land, they carried their religious scrolls and their history with them, otherwise they would have lost their sense of who they were. We need our history, all of us."

"Dad, do you know about Dunkirk?"

His father gave him a comic look of amazement. "Of course."

"And Suez?"

"I was only four when Dunkirk happened, but I was *well* around for Suez. Neither of them were glorious British victories exactly. But you have to know about them."

"Will you tell me?"

"Yes. I'd love to. First we do this."

He set the cupboard carefully, almost ceremonially, on Omri's desk. Omri picked up the wampum belt very carefully by one of its tiny fringed ends and laid it on the shelf.

"They've had a week," his dad said. "I've been following their trek on a map, thinking where they could have got to, each day. . . . If nothing terrible's happened, they could have crossed the border by now, beyond the reach of the settlers. If only we could be sure!"

"I just hope this belt goes back to its owner, and not to the place it came from."

"Mightn't it be better to bring Little Bear back and just give it to him?" his dad said. Omri could see the eagerness in his eyes.

"No, Dad. We can't bring them back anymore."

His father's face fell. "You mean, never?"

"No. Mum agrees."

His father was stunned and couldn't speak at first. *"Mum . . . knows?"*

"Dad. Are you surprised?"

After a long moment, he shook his head. "I did wonder," he said. "Especially when she seemed to swallow all that guff of Patrick's, and didn't twig about Gillon's dream. I'm glad. It's gone right against the grain, keeping it a secret from her. But of course, I should have known. She has the gift, too. . . . And she says—we're to stop?"

Omri nodded. His dad heaved a great sigh.

"You know best, Om. Both of you. I'm going to miss them, though!"

They took a last look at the belt which was their final link. Then Omri closed the cupboard door and turned the key. While they were standing there, *willing* the belt to go back to wherever Little Bear was now, Omri suddenly said: "Dad, guess my dream."

His father looked at him in amazement.

"Like the Indians do?"

"Yes."

"I don't know how."

"If you try to guess, then I can tell you."

"You—you dreamt they got there safe, and—"

"No. I dreamt I was in some kind of battle. The soldiers around me were Indians. Someone was shooting at us. And I had nothing but a pencil in my hand. And I heard Little Bear's voice say, 'We are of one mind.'"

"Well, I don't know, bub. Perhaps, with your gift, you foresaw something that's up ahead for you, something— to do with the Indians. In the future. Listen, it's good. It shows they're going to be around a long time, still fighting battles for their people. The Canada option was never going to be easy."

"What about the pencil? I wanted it to be a gun but it wasn't."

"Guns don't settle anything; they just kill people. They say the pen is mightier than the sword or the gun. A pencil could be just as mighty as a pen."

Omri wasn't clear what he meant. But he was comforted. He opened the cupboard again, took the tiny plastic strip out, wrapped it in a scrap of paper, and put it away in the cashbox. Just before he closed it, his dad said, "Put this in, too. Otherwise *I* might be tempted."

And he laid the magic car key in the cashbox.

As he closed the lid, a gust of wind blew through the open window. Omri raised his head. "Smell that, Dad?"

"What?"

"Like new hay. Only it can't be, not in October."

"So what is it? I can't smell anything."

"It's sweetgrass," Omri said. A grin of pure pleasure lit up his face. "Bright Stars is making a basket. They got there."